W9-BOL-837

DANCY'S WOMAN

**Center Point
Large Print**

Also by Lori Copeland and available from Center Point Large Print:

Twice Loved
Three Times Blessed
Someone to Love
Tall Cotton
One True Love

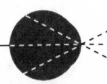

**This Large Print Book carries the
Seal of Approval of N.A.V.H.**

DANCY'S WOMAN

Lori Copeland

CENTER POINT PUBLISHING
THORNDIKE, MAINE

This Center Point Large Print edition
is published in the year 2011 by arrangement with
Lori Copeland, Inc.

The text of this Large Print edition is unabridged.
In other aspects, this book may vary
from the original edition.
Printed in the United States of America
on permanent paper.
Set in 16-point Times New Roman type.

ISBN: 978-1-60285-976-0

Library of Congress Cataloging-in-Publication Data

Copeland, Lori.
Dancy's woman / Lori Copeland.
p. cm.
ISBN 978-1-60285-976-0 (lib. bdg. : alk. paper)
1. Large type books. I. Title.
PS3553.O6336D36 2011
813′.54—dc22

2010037402

To Evan Marshall—
one terrific agent

Chapter One

OUT OF THE blue, the alarm sounded.

Lauren froze, stunned by the high, piercing squeal that suddenly shattered the silence of the room. Her startled eyes scanned the terminal board before her as she studied the various gauges with growing apprehension.

She edged forward on her chair, watching as the pressure on line four plummeted rapidly.

"I'm losing unit four at Gulfport on number one south." Lauren spoke calmly, but her tone belied the sudden apprehension squeezing her throat.

She shot a warning look to her co-worker, Sam Moyers, who was seated at the console next to hers. If she had to shut the unit down, Sam would have to follow suit on his terminal, too.

Sam lifted his sandy brows expectantly and peered over the rim of his wire frames at Lauren. "Are you in trouble?"

Lauren watched silently as the pressure unit on one continued to fall.

Cooper Vandis's head snapped up when the alarm sounded. Cooper wasn't new to the everyday workings of a pipeline terminal; he'd been in the business since he was a kid. However, until six months ago, he'd never owned his own company, so today the unexpected alarm had a more menacing sound to it. Cooper pushed back his chair and stood. A frown creased his rugged features. "What's wrong?"

"I'm not sure. . . ." Lauren answered hesitantly. The remaining gauges on her console were functioning normally. Only the pressure gauge on unit four was falling.

Cooper covered the space between his desk and Lauren's console seemingly effortlessly for a man who would be sixty years old the coming spring. His tall, athletic frame dominated the room as he stood behind his daughter's chair. His eyes shrewdly assessed the situation.

"What are you running on four?" he asked briskly.

"Crude."

They watched as the pressure on the line continued to fall at an alarming rate.

"We've got a rupture somewhere." Cooper made his decision abruptly. "Shut it down."

Sam Moyers flashed a quick glance at Lauren before reaching to shut down his unit.

Cooper swore under his breath as he fumbled in his pocket for a Lucky Strike.

Coyle Dancy's day hadn't started out the best. When he'd come out of the house that morning, his backhoe had a dead battery; when he'd gone to feed, he'd discovered the oil pump was out on the old pickup, and when he'd made his morning rounds, he'd found close to thirty dead fry floating on top of the rearing ponds. To top it off, a filling had dropped out of a back molar while he'd chewed the biscuits he'd overcooked for breakfast that morning.

It hadn't been the first time Coyle had seriously considered having his head examined. He'd been warned that raising catfish wasn't the most lucrative nor the easiest way to make a buck, but he'd paid no attention to skeptics.

Coyle had made up his mind that there had to be a better way to make a living than spending his life driving an eighteen-wheeler cross-country, and he'd meant to find it.

He had thought a thirty-year-old man should be laying down roots instead of hauling them.

So, when an opportunity to purchase fifty acres of prime land just outside Picayune, Mississippi, had come along, Coyle had withdrawn every cent he'd saved for fifteen years, and, as his friends liked to describe it, "he'd lost his cotton-pickin' mind!"

Certain that only a fool would've passed it up, Coyle had bought the land. With three spring-fed ponds and two deep wells, he'd figured the land would be perfect for raising catfish.

Coyle had thought that in a couple of years he could quit the road and settle down to a normal life-style.

He'd taken his friends' good-natured ribbing in stride as he'd applied for an FHA loan. Later he'd started building ponds and buying equipment. Realizing he needed to know more about fish, he'd enrolled in night school and proceeded to learn everything he could about ichthyology.

It hadn't take Coyle long to discover that a catfish farmer had to know more than how catfish live, reproduce, and grow. He had to learn how to select the most desirable fish, keep disease and parasites under control, provide the proper feed, manage the water, harvest and market the fish, and cope with managerial problems.

Not an easy chore for a truck driver with a basic high school education, but because Coyle believed that he could do it, he'd plunged headlong into his new venture, thriving on a heady dose of optimism and ignoring the pessimists.

At times Coyle had admitted that it hadn't been as easy as he'd hoped. And he was sure thankful that he'd never married.

He'd come close once, but he'd backed out at the last minute. Susan's goals had been different from his, and they'd both realized it in time. Later Coyle had been glad that he hadn't put a woman through all he'd had to face during the past few years.

Right now, the money was tighter than a fat woman's girdle on Sunday morning, but Coyle was determined to make it. Success was just around the corner, and he could practically smell it.

Come fall, he'd have his first big harvest. He'd bet that his friends would be singing a different tune then. The cheery prediction lifted Coyle's sagging spirits as he backed his old Ford into the shed. As he connected the jumper cables to the battery in the backhoe, Coyle assured himself that although his day had started off badly, the worst was over.

In minutes Coyle had the backhoe engine running. He climbed aboard, bemoaning the fact his whole morning would be devoted to digging a small ditch so he could install a drainage culvert along the south fencerow.

He'd put it off as long as he could; now it had to be finished before he could leave on another haul late this evening. The standing water from recent rains had become not only a nuisance, but an eyesore as well.

He shoved the backhoe into gear and drove to the fence line, glancing fretfully to the west. Another storm was brewing, and he needed to get the pipe installed before the rain moved in.

Coyle edged the tractor along the fencerow, pausing later beside a large, nasty-looking pool of water.

Yes, Coyle thought absently as he lowered the shovel down to touch the rain-sodden earth, when his friends got a load of the money he'd make from this year's harvest, they'd change their attitudes. They'd laughed and teased him about moving from bustling L.A. to slow-moving Picayune. Where in the *devil* is Picayune, Mississippi? had been their favorite jibe, and Coyle had patiently explained that Picayune was a small town in the heart of the Sunbelt, not far from the excitement and gaiety of New Orleans. Coyle planned to show them that Picayune, Mississippi, could produce some of the best catfish—

KER-BLAMMMMM!

Dirt flew into Coyle's eyes, and he saw stars explode as he felt what seemed like an atomic explosion beneath his seat before being hurled helplessly through the air like a rag doll.

About the time Sam was shutting down unit four, Lauren was doing the same. Just moments before, the line had carried crude oil from Georgia to Mississippi through thousands of miles of underground pipe.

Lauren hoped her father was mistaken and that there was some other explanation for the disruption on unit four. But if there had been a rupture, she prayed that she hadn't been the cause of it.

She sprang from her chair and hurried to read the printout that reviewed the line's pressures every forty seconds.

Scanning the sheet carefully, she searched to determine if she'd been the one in error.

Moments later, she breathed a sigh of relief when she was able to confirm that all her gauges were open, that the products were going where they should, and that all of her pressure readings were well within tolerance levels.

If there had been a rupture, the pipe had sprung a leak on its own.

Walking back to her console, she wished again that she was back at her old job. At least she'd be more comfortable with her work.

For the past seven years she'd been a nurse in a cardiac care unit. Her becoming a pipeline dispatcher had been Cooper's idea.

Oh, she'd been around the business all her life, but when Cooper purchased the pipeline six months before, he'd insisted that Lauren quit her job at the hospital and train in every aspect of the everyday experiences of operating a pipeline terminal.

Cooper reasoned that Lauren would someday inherit Vandis Pipelines—not that she wanted it. Lauren had made that known on numerous occasions, but Cooper was a fanatic about making certain that his only child would be well taken care of in the event of his death.

Lauren tried to understand her father, reminding herself that since he'd suffered his second heart attack in as many years, Cooper was convinced he would die prematurely, even though the doctors had told him that if he'd slow down and throw away the cigarettes he smoked incessantly, he would increase his chances of living long enough to hold his grandchildren.

But Cooper was hardheaded—endearing, but hardheaded. Four years before, he'd lost the love of his life, Jenny, his wife and Lauren's mother. Since then, Cooper had lived his life exactly as he wanted.

Lauren knew Cooper wasn't concerned about the physical aspects of dying; he just wanted to make sure he had everything in order before he—as he colorfully termed it—checked out.

Despite Cooper's ambitions for her, Lauren had faced facts: as a nurse, she was competent, but as a business manager, she was a real washout.

Her desk was cluttered with bills that needed to be paid, correspondence that begged to be answered, invoices that required immediate attention.

And today, instead of getting completely caught up as she'd planned, she'd had to fill in for Walt Musky, who'd awakened this morning with a debilitating case of intestinal flu.

Lauren was always uneasy about working

dispatch. Although she'd mastered that area of the business, the pressure still made her nervous.

Transmitting the flow of liquids through pipelines was handled in much the same way that the movement of trains was controlled on a railroad. One false move could spell disaster.

She knew only too well a crude oil spill was a nasty occurrence. The Environmental Protection Agency would have to be notified, and the waste would have to be cleaned up as quickly as possible. Lauren didn't want to think about the possible personal injuries that might have been a result of such an accident. She had one fervent hope—if a pipe had ruptured, she prayed that it had happened in an isolated area where no one could have been hurt.

Cooper returned to his desk and dialed the division office. His call was answered on the second ring.

"Jack, looks like we've got a problem," Cooper relayed in a clipped tone.

Lauren kept a close eye on the remaining lines in operation, listening as her father quickly explained the situation. State-of-the-art technology made it possible to alert all on-duty pipeline personnel of a crisis so they could respond quickly with necessary data.

Seconds later Cooper hung up and walked over to study a map that covered most of one wall. Hundreds of multicolored dots pinpointed the vast network of underground pipelines snaking across the United States.

Cooper began running his index finger along the routes, talking to himself, an annoying, yet endearing habit to which his co-workers had grown accustomed. Abruptly his finger stopped, and he mumbled around the cigarette hanging from the corner of his mouth, "Where in the *heck* is Picayune, Mississippi?"

"Picayune, Mississippi?" Lauren shrugged her narrow shoulders. "I'm not sure. . . . Why?"

"Looks like that's where our trouble is." Cooper studied the map and discovered that Picayune was a small town close to New Orleans.

After striding back to the phone, Cooper punched out another number. Lauren overheard him asking the operator to connect him with the county sheriff's office in Picayune.

Minutes later a grim-faced Cooper dropped the receiver back on the hook. "It's a rupture, all right. There's at least one injury."

The frightening ramifications of an accident of this magnitude made Lauren's head swim.

Naturally the company was insured. She'd paid the renewal policy only last month, but sometimes the coverage was not nearly enough in cases like this one, and a huge, lengthy lawsuit would be the last thing her father needed now, especially when he was trying to get the business off to a smooth start.

"Did he say how serious the injury was?" Lauren asked.

"The sheriff wasn't sure. He said the rupture had occurred on the outskirts of Picayune. There's still a lot of confusion about what took place." Cooper ran his hands distractedly through the wiry crop of white hair scattered sparsely atop his head. He took another long drag from his cigarette. "I'd better notify the insurance company and get Burke down there right away." He ground out his cigarette and lit another.

Burke Hunter had been a friend of the Vandis family for years. When Cooper had bought the business, he'd automatically asked the young, up-and-coming lawyer to represent Vandis Pipelines. Lauren felt sure Burke could handle the situation efficiently—if he were available.

"Burke's out of town, Dad."

"Out of town? Where is he?"

"Somewhere in Alaska, I think."

"Alaska!" Cooper looked stunned.

"I'm afraid so," Lauren said. "Burke phoned last week and mentioned that he was taking Mary Beth Whitley on a two-week cruise up the Pacific Coast to Alaska."

"Doesn't that boy ever stay home?" Cooper muttered irritably, as he strode toward his desk to snatch the shrilling phone off its hook.

Lauren shrugged. How Burke Hunter spent his private time was of no concern to her.

"Vandis here!"

"We're on top of the situation," Jack Matthews, the division manager relayed. "The foreman and his crew are on their way to the scene. Looks like we've got a real mess on our hands, Coop."

"Is the rupture small enough to throw a saddle over?"

"Doesn't sound like it. From what little I know, it seems someone was digging and hit the pipe. Sounds like the whole section's going to have to be replaced."

"Do you know anything about the injuries?"

"Not much," Jack admitted, "just that the victim's on his way to the hospital. We'll have a crew at the site in ten minutes or so. I'll know more then."

Cooper sighed wearily. "Thanks, Jack. Keep in touch."

"Will do."

Replacing the receiver slowly, Cooper turned to face Lauren.

"You'd better call Al and have him come in early."

Lauren nodded as Cooper prepared to file a report on the leak. "Oh, and Lauren," he said casually, "I think you'd better plan on going down there."

Lauren glanced up from her terminal. "Where?"

"To Picayune."

Until five minutes ago she hadn't even been aware that there *was* a Picayune, Mississippi, and now she certainly didn't feel any burning desire to visit there. The town's name alone seemed to discourage the thought. "Why?"

"Well, since Burke's not available, I want you to hop a plane and get down there to represent us."

"You want me to go to Picayune?" Lauren thought she'd heard everything in the past six months, but Cooper's newest request topped them all.

"Someone has to go, and I'll be tied up here trying to get things under control."

"What am I supposed to do once I get there?"

"Soothe egos, Lauren. Assure the injured party that we're doing all we can to take care of this spill. Hey, kiss a few egos if you have to. I want to keep a lawsuit down to the minimum," Cooper confessed, realizing that that would be about as unlikely as a balmy January day at The North Pole, but he wanted to try.

"Dad . . . don't you think you should send someone experienced in this sort of thing instead of me?" Lauren protested, knowing only too well that she wasn't a diplomat.

At times, even she thought she was scatterbrained, and Cooper had no doubt about it. So why would he send her on such a crucial mission? she wondered.

"There's no one else I can send, Lauren," Cooper admitted, smiling at her encouragingly through a veil of blue smoke. "I'll put in a call to Burke while you're packing. Surely he left a number where he can be reached. Meanwhile, you get on down to Picayune and make sure the family of the injured party knows we're not some hard-nosed outfit that doesn't give a hoot."

Cooper Vandis was a businessman, but he was a compassionate man, too. If his pipeline had been responsible for the rupture, then he'd make good on the damages, even if it had to come out of his own pocket.

Lauren sighed and walked toward her desk as Cooper replaced her at the terminal. "I don't like it. I'll only go down there and make things worse," Lauren predicted.

"I have every faith you won't. All I want you to do is make sure the injured know we're on top of this. Our insurance should take care of it, but I don't want an additional lawsuit slapped on me if I can prevent it."

Lauren picked up the phone and called Al Watson; she informed him of the emergency and asked him to report to work as soon as possible. Al agreed to be there in thirty minutes.

As she reached for her purse, Lauren's eyes focused on the stack of unpaid bills lying on her desk. Suddenly her stomach did a queer flip-flop.

She *had* mailed the payment for the insurance renewal—hadn't she?

Cooper glanced up from the terminal and saw her face grow suddenly pale. "What's wrong, Tooters?" he asked.

Tooters was Cooper's affectionate childhood term for his daughter, which, to her dismay, he still used regularly. The nickname had first originated when Lauren received a horn from Santa on her fourth Christmas. She had played it day and night until, much to her parents' relief, she permanently misplaced it one day; henceforth the name Tooters had haunted her ever since.

Lauren snapped out of her startled reverie and smiled. "Nothing."

"Then you'd better get going. You should be able to get a plane out of here within the hour. Call me the minute you get down there and let me know how bad the injuries are."

"Sure . . . first thing." Lauren scooped up the stack of overdue bills and discreetly jammed them into her coat pocket.

Of course she had paid the insurance renewal bill, she assured herself again as she hurried out to her car.

"*Please,* Lord," she whispered, "let me at least have paid that one bill."

But as soon as she got inside the car, she pulled the thick stack of envelopes from her pocket and began rifling through them. Suddenly she froze. The long yellow envelope from the insurance agency stared back at her menacingly. FINAL NOTICE.

Her heart dropped to her knees. Dear Lord, she hadn't paid the bill. How could anyone be so irresponsible? she agonized.

Well, how did Cooper expect her to keep up with these things! She'd *told* him she was a miserable wretch when it came to bookkeeping!

But there it was in black and white. The notice clearly stated that their payment was due on the fifteenth of June.

Lifting her wrist, Lauren pressed the date button on her watch and shut her eyes. Her stomach felt queasy as she forced her eyes to reopen slowly.

Today was the twelfth of August. Their payment was almost two months past due; their coverage was terminated.

Chapter Two

A LITTLE OVER three hours later, the Boeing 727 landed at New Orleans International Airport. Lauren carried her small overnight bag from the plane and headed for the first telephone booth she could find. From there, it took her only a moment to look up the address of Picayune's hospital. Rummaging through her purse, she located a deposit slip and scribbled the address across it.

Minutes later Lauren was outside, hailing a cab to take her the sixty-five miles to the hospital. When she arrived at the entrance, she saw a modern, attractive building that, judging from its size, must have had fewer than a hundred and fifty beds. It couldn't be too difficult to find the injured party, Lauren thought. As she paid the driver, she noticed an entrance to her right. Assuming the injured person might still be receiving emergency treatment, Lauren decided to check there first.

It didn't take long for her to find him. As she entered the hospital, Lauren cringed at the harsh sound of an angry masculine voice shouting his displeasure over the unfortunate turn of events.

His voice echoed loudly up and down the corridors. "I want the name of the moron responsible for this outrage—and I want it now!"

Lauren timidly made her way down the hall, trying to maintain her composure as she listened to the dire predictions coming through the closed and forbidding entrance to emergency.

The resounding threats against the responsible culprit continued, ranging from his promise to shoot him point-blank with a four-ten shotgun to his vow to personally castrate him with a dull knife. Lauren found neither alternative particularly appealing.

Suddenly, a nurse shot through the double doors, her demeanor clearly shaken as she scurried down the hallway.

Hoping that she was mistaken and that the man in the emergency room was not the one she was looking for, Lauren hesitantly stepped forward to intercept the flustered nurse. "Excuse me. . . . I'm looking for the one who was injured in the pipeline explosion."

The nurse shot her a look of disbelief and barely took the time to acknowledge her meek inquiry. "Coyle Dancy? He's in there," the nurse said over her shoulder, briefly gesturing toward the emergency room as she rushed down the hallway.

Lauren's heart sank as the male voice raged on furiously. It was Coyle Dancy's voice—the one she had been sent to soothe, Lauren realized sickly.

Unsure as to what to do next, Lauren glanced around, noticing for the first time that the small waiting room was empty. The television perched on a high shelf was broadcasting the evening news. The cold remains in two Styrofoam coffee cups attested to someone's earlier presence. Members of Mr. Dancy's family, Lauren surmised. If so, she rationalized, perhaps she should talk with them first.

But no one was around. Magazines and newspapers littered the room, along with ashtrays overflowing with cigarette butts and wads of discarded chewing gum.

The nurses' station looked empty. The ward was deserted except for an occasional feminine voice mingled with abrupt and irritable outbursts from Mr. Dancy.

Edging her way to the emergency room doors, Lauren tried to peek inside, but the glass windows were too high for her. The rustle of a uniform as a nurse approached made her jump guiltily. The nurse rushed past Lauren and entered the double doors with brisk professionalism.

Well, what should I do now, Lauren thought. Coyle Dancy didn't sound like he was in the mood for company, and she wondered again how she had let Cooper talk her into this.

Her eyes located the telephone, and she hurried over to place a call to Vandis Pipelines. Perhaps if she explained to Cooper that seeing Coyle

Dancy really wasn't wise, he'd agree to let her return home.

Actually, Lauren felt that Attila the Hun would be better suited to soothe Mr. Dancy's ruffled feathers, not a scatterbrained girl like herself, whose knees already felt like glue.

"Dad? I'm here."

"What have you been able to find out?"

"Not much. I'm at the hospital now."

"How serious are the injuries?"

"As far as I can tell, one man was injured . . . but I don't think his condition is life-threatening." Lauren recoiled again as she heard another belligerent bellow from the emergency room.

"Thank God—that's a relief," Cooper acknowledged.

"At least the injuries haven't affected Mr. Dancy's lungs," she added.

"Dancy? Is he the injured party?"

"Yes. Dad, I think we better reconsider my talking with Mr. Dancy. I have a hunch he isn't in the mood to listen to apologies."

"Make them anyway," Cooper ordered. "I was able to reach Burke. He's flying home immediately, but he can't get a plane out until morning. You assure Mr. Dancy that Vandis Pipelines has adequate insurance, and we'll have a crew out at his place in another couple of hours to start the cleanup."

Lauren felt ill as she thought of the lapsed

insurance policy still in her coat pocket. How would she ever explain her incompetence? Yet, he had to know. "Dad—"

"No buts, Tooters. You've got to handle this. I haven't got time to stand around and chew the fat. Do what I sent you down there for and call me back when you find out the extent of Dancy's injuries." Lauren heard the familiar flick of Cooper's lighter.

"Dad, you're smoking too much—"

Cooper wasn't in the mood for reprimands. "Call me back the minute you know something." The connection went dead.

"But, Dad," Lauren continued, as if Cooper were still on the line, "I forgot to pay the insurance notice." Somehow admitting it eased her conscience, even though she knew her father wasn't listening.

Lauren imagined Cooper's kindly voice responding in a gentle, understanding fashion. "Lauren . . . Lauren, don't worry about a thing. I know you're a fool. Jenny and I had to live with that fact for years, but you're my daughter, Tooters, and I love you. Anyone could have made the same mistake."

"Thanks, Dad. . . . I really meant to pay the bill," Lauren said, still foolishly fantasizing.

Feeling greatly relieved, Lauren replaced the receiver and stood for a moment, leaning against the phone booth.

You *are* an idiot, she reminded herself coldly. When Cooper really learned she hadn't paid the policy, daughter or not, he was going to skin her alive and nail her remains to a telephone pole somewhere in outer Siberia. How long would it take for the insurance company to discover her mistake? There was no way of knowing.

Lauren had no idea how long she would have stayed within the security of the phone booth if an older man hadn't walked up and tapped at the door.

Apologizing briefly, Lauren headed back toward the emergency room as a young man came through the double doors carrying a covered tray.

"Excuse me. Are you a doctor?" Lauren hurried to his side.

The young man paused. "Afraid not. I'm just an orderly," Dan Mercer admitted.

"Oh . . . I was wondering about Mr. Dancy. How is he?"

"Coyle?" Dan flashed a winning smile, boldly admiring the outline of the great set of legs displayed in Lauren's Calvin Kleins. "It'll be a few minutes before you can see Coyle. They're still working on him, but he's as tough as a boot."

"Exactly how serious are his injuries?" Lauren asked hesitantly.

Dan's left brow lifted suspiciously. "Hasn't the doctor talked to you yet?"

"Oh . . . yes, but I thought you could *really* tell me how Coyle is coming along."

"Real good for what he's been through. A blow like that would've killed most men, but Coyle's like a Timex," Dan conceded.

Lauren stared back at him blankly.

"You know . . . one of those Timex watches? He takes a lickin' and keeps on tickin'?"

"Oh . . . yes." Lauren smiled lamely. "How lucky for Mr. Dancy."

"I'd say," Dan continued. "That explosion could have blown his tail off. Boy, whoever's responsible for puttin' that pipeline in and leaving it unmarked is dead meat. You know what I mean?"

Lauren cleared her throat nervously. She did, only too well. "Then Mr. Dancy's hospital stay will probably be lengthy?"

"No. They're gonna send him home in the morning if everything else checks out all right. Even though he's got a broken leg, a bunch of cuts and bruises, and a couple busted ribs, the doctor says he can recuperate at home." Dan gave her an apologetic look and started edging down the hallway after a nurse passed them and shot him a warning glance. "Don't worry your pretty head none, ma'am. Coyle's being taken care of real good. If you'll just hang around for a few minutes, one of the nurses will let you in to see him."

Lauren smiled. "Thank you."

The orderly hurried away as Lauren breathed an audible sigh of relief. Thank goodness, Dancy's injuries weren't serious. Since the doctor was sending Dancy home in the morning, she reasoned he'd probably be in a better mood to listen to apologies then.

Lauren's spirits brightened. That's it, she thought. She wouldn't approach the man today. She'd wait until he was comfortably settled into his familiar surroundings, and then she'd make the required explanations and assurances.

By then the cleanup crews would be on site, and Mr. Dancy would be able to see for himself that Vandis Pipelines was in full control of the situation.

With a little luck, Mr. Dancy would even be able to shed new light on the mysterious explosion. If some sort of digging had been involved, as Jack had mentioned earlier, then it was entirely possible that Mr. Dancy was the one at fault. Lauren prayed that would be the case.

Cooper wasn't a rich man, and a large lawsuit above the actual damages could devastate him.

Lauren couldn't bear to face the fact that her incompetence would be the cause of such a disaster. She had to find a way to prevent a lawsuit . . . though she had no idea how they could avoid one if the accident resulted from negligence on the part of Vandis Pipelines.

In any case, they wouldn't starve. If the worst happened, Lauren vowed to personally see to it that Cooper was taken care of comfortably for the rest of his life, even if it meant she'd have to work double shifts at the hospital.

Postponing her meeting with Coyle Dancy until the following morning would mean having to spend the night in Picayune, but Lauren supposed she'd manage.

As a precaution, she'd thrown a pair of pajamas and a toothbrush into her overnight case, so staying over wouldn't be that inconvenient. She'd rent a motel room; the overnight delay would give her time to plan a strategy.

Maybe she was borrowing trouble. Maybe Mr. Dancy would turn out to be a kindly old gentleman who would be rather understanding once she explained her predicament, she thought hopefully.

There were a few nice people left in the world, and, with a modicum of luck Coyle Dancy would prove to be one of them. Lauren stiffened as she heard the now familiar male voice shout another loud obscenity.

Then again, she thought, maybe Coyle Dancy was as heartless as he sounded. That was a possibility Lauren didn't even want to consider.

At any rate, she would wait until tomorrow to approach him. Her decision firmly made, Lauren felt somewhat relieved.

Perhaps by then Mr. Dancy's wife or his children would be around. Maybe it would be best to speak to them first. She decided to make that decision after she'd rented a room and taken a cool shower.

Heading back toward the exit, Lauren paused as she overheard two nurses whispering as they came out of the emergency room.

"I'd be willing to take a leave of absence to get the job," one of the nurses confessed with a breathless giggle. "I'd love to get my hands on Coyle Dancy . . . if you know what I mean."

"You and thirty other women," the second one agreed. "He's acting perfectly dreadful, but I'd love to have the chance to calm him down."

"Oh no you don't! I want to be the one to take the starch out of the little devil's tail." The first one winked. "If *you* know what I mean."

They giggled again as they disappeared down the hall.

Lauren pushed through the heavy door and went outside, puzzled by their exchange.

"Where to, lady?" The cabbie peered at her in the rearview mirror as she climbed into the backseat of a waiting taxi.

"The nearest motel . . . a clean one," she added. She'd do about anything for Cooper, except fight roaches and limp feather pillows all night.

"Yes, ma'am." The cabbie pulled out onto the street as Lauren settled against the seat to glance out the windows. The residents of Picayune appeared to take pride in their town, providing ample schools, churches, and shopping facilities.

The two giggling nurses surfaced in Lauren's mind again. They both had wanted a shot at nursing Coyle Dancy back to health. Did that mean he wasn't married? she wondered. Widowed? Yes, that was probably it. He was probably a widower who needed nursing care until he was fully recovered.

Lauren sighed. The man couldn't be all that bad if two nurses were fussing over who might get the job, she consoled herself.

Coyle Dancy was probably filthy rich, a crusty, old coot who'd be more than anxious to have some young, good-looking nurse around to rub his back and give him sponge baths.

Lauren peered pensively at the passing scenery. Still, she had a nagging feeling that she wasn't going to like him, not unless he was an old, rich coot who was exceptionally understanding and forgiving.

Well, she decided, the following day would reveal the real Coyle Dancy.

The cab pulled up in front of the motel, and Lauren paid the fare. Her room turned out to be bright and cheerful, and she headed immediately for the shower.

Twenty minutes later she called room service and ordered coffee and a turkey sandwich.

Deciding she'd put off calling her father for as long as she could, she placed a call to his office and listened to the phone ring four times. She was about to hang up when Cooper finally answered.

"Dad?"

"Yeah?"

"I was about to hang up. Are you still working?"

"Afraid so. What's going on there?"

"Nothing. I've decided to stay overnight and talk to Mr. Dancy in the morning."

"Why?"

"He was still in the emergency room, and I didn't think that was the time or the place to carry on a conversation."

"Did you contact his family?"

"I didn't see anyone around."

"How bad are his injuries?"

"A broken leg, fractured ribs, and a few cuts and bruises. But I understand they're going to release him in the morning."

"No kidding?" Cooper sounded relieved. "That sounds good. I guess you're right. It might be wiser to talk to him in the morning."

"Have you found out anything new about the accident?"

"Yeah, seems Dancy was digging some sort of a ditch when he hit the line."

"Wasn't the line marked?"

"It should have been. I don't know what

happened. All I know is we have a nasty spill to clean up. Dancy has a catfish farm, and it looks like he's suffered some pretty heavy losses. We're going to try to recover as much as we can. The dozers are out there building a dike around the ponds right now, but it looks like some of the soil will have to be dug up and hauled away."

Lauren was heartsick as she heard the weariness in her father's voice. "Oh, Dad . . . I'm so sorry."

"Don't worry about it, baby. It's just one of those things. At least no one was killed. . . . We'll let the insurance company worry about the rest."

"Dad . . ." Lauren had to tell him about the lapsed policy. It was only a matter of time before he discovered that they weren't covered.

"Yes?"

Lauren's courage began to wilt. A little more time, that's all she needed. She probably had a few more hours before Cooper found out she hadn't paid the policy. Until then, she would stall.

First she would assess Coyle Dancy's attitude. Perhaps if he were reasonable, she and Burke could work out an amicable settlement before Cooper found out. If the settlement was a good one, maybe it would help soften the inevitable blow.

"You'd better go home and get some rest," she cautioned.

"I have a few more things to wrap up here, then I'll head that way. Call me in the morning after you've contacted Dancy. Burke should be in by late tomorrow afternoon."

"Sure, Dad. First thing."

"Lauren, now don't you be up half the night worrying. That's why we have insurance, for emergencies like this. You hear?"

"I hear."

Lauren replaced the receiver and stared at the remains of her half-eaten sandwich. When he found out, Cooper would never forgive her. She couldn't blame him; she'd never be able to forgive herself.

Chapter Three

❖ ❖ ❖

"MR. DANCY, HOW NICE to meet you. My name is Lauren Vandis. My father, Cooper Vandis—the man who's responsible for the pipeline you happened to encounter unexpectedly . . ."

Wincing, Lauren pitched her hairbrush onto the vanity and stared back at her reflection in the mirror sternly. That sounded horrible.

She cleared her throat. "Mr. Dancy," she began with a big, bright smile, "I do hope you're feeling better today. Lovely weather for the middle of August, don't you agree?"

No, she decided, that sounded more ridiculous than the first attempt. It was only a few minutes past eight o'clock, and the temperature was already hovering at ninety-five degrees. She could practically wring the humidity out of the air, and Lauren was sure that a man with a broken leg, two broken ribs, and numerous stitches over his body would not agree that the weather was lovely.

"Mr. Dancy," she said, using a crisp, professional voice this time. "My name is Lauren Vandis—I'm representing Vandis Pipelines. I've been sent to Picayune to make sure that you're resting comfortably and receiving the best of care. I want to assure you that we will do everything within our power to . . ."

Her voice trailed off when she realized that this approach wouldn't work either. Such a wimpy statement would imply that Vandis Pipelines was the party at fault, which was still uncertain.

Lauren sighed. She couldn't think straight without her first cup of coffee. Maybe something brilliant would occur to her during breakfast.

Before leaving the motel, Lauren called home again. Cooper relayed the grim news that the pipes that had ruptured were so old that they couldn't be repaired. This would require more delay while the repair crew laid a network of new underground lines.

"Dad, are you taking care of yourself?" With each conversation, Lauren could hear more fatigue creeping into Cooper's tone.

"I'm fine." The unrelenting flick of a lighter followed his preoccupied denial.

"You're smoking too much." Lauren knew how much Cooper hated to be reminded, but, because his health was at stake, she was determined to keep after him anyway.

"I'm fine."

"Coffin nails, Dad, that's what they are."

"We all have our vices, Tooters. Now get to work."

The story of the ruptured pipeline dominated the headlines of the *Times-Picayune*: PIPELINE RUPTURE INJURES AREA MAN AND LEAVES LARGE TOXIC SPILL.

The morning crowd had gathered in the diner, eager to hear more details of the accident. Over coffee and juice, Lauren studied the various accounts of the accident, while keeping one ear turned to the television located behind the counter. An area news station had minicams on the spot, conducting interviews with anyone they could corner.

"Sir . . . sir . . . excuse me, I understand you witnessed the explosion yesterday morning?" A pretty female reporter thrust a microphone in the face of an elderly man who wore a New Orleans Saints baseball cap.

Pausing, the man glanced about nervously until, certain that the cameras were rolling, he began haltingly, "Well . . . yes, ma'am . . . I shore did."

"Can you tell us about it?" The microphone moved closer as the camera crew edged forward.

"Well"—the man cleared his throat anxiously—"I was just passin' by the Dancy place on my way to town yesterday when all of a sudden it sounded like one of them atomic bombs had done gone off."

"Did you see Mr. Dancy?"

The man spat tobacco onto the ground as he began to bask in the warmth of the limelight. "Shore did. Seen him a-flying through the air like one of them trapeze artists, only I knew there warn't no net there to catch him when he landed."

"And the damages. What would you assess to be the damages to Mr. Dancy's farm?"

"Well, I don't know, but I'd say it's pert near wiped ole Coyle out." The man shook his head sadly. "Shore has. It's a real shame, too. He's worked real hard to get this place producin', but it's all gone now." The man looked over his shoulder expectantly. "Why, there's hundreds . . . maybe thousands of fish floatin' dead on them ponds. Shore is a shame. Right pitiful, actually."

By this time Lauren had left her table and wedged herself in at the counter. She watched with growing horror as the camera panned the region, giving the viewers a sobering look at the magnitude of the destruction. The area was teeming with frenzied activity as crews worked to repair the rupture and contain the spill.

Lauren closed her eyes wearily as the reporter began to summarize the gruesome details. Poor Mr. Dancy, she agonized. The man had had more than his share of trouble.

"Jill," said the news anchor at the station, interrupting the reporter's rambling commentary.

"Yes, Phil?"

"Have you received an update from the hospital on Coyle Dancy's condition?"

Frowning, Jill pressed her forefinger to the microphone hooked to her ear. She seemed to be having difficulty hearing his question. "Phil, a hospital spokesman released a statement about ten minutes ago that Mr. Dancy would be dismissed sometime today," she reported. "Apparently, his injuries are not as severe as first thought, which will certainly be good news to our viewers."

"That is good news, Jill. We'll return to you at the site in about thirty minutes for another update on the crisis."

"Thanks, Phil." Jill was still smiling as the regularly scheduled *Today Show* returned to the screen.

Feeling numb, Lauren shuffled back to her table and watched as the waitress set her breakfast in front of her. It was clear that this accident was becoming monumental in scope.

Refilling the advertised bottomless coffee cup, the waitress frowned absently. "Everyone in Picayune sure likes Coyle Dancy. I sure hope whoever's responsible for this catastrophe will be held accountable."

Lauren nodded in lame agreement before turning her attention to the plate of scrambled eggs and bacon. Though the food smelled tempting, Lauren had lost her appetite.

The waitress tucked her order pad into her pocket and shrugged. "Just whistle if you need anything, sugar."

Would that offer happen to include a large insurance policy? Lauren thought wryly.

With a sigh, she reached into her purse for the

money to pay the bill. She'd procrastinated long enough. It was time she met Coyle Dancy and saw for herself what a wonderful and, she fervently hoped, rational man he actually was.

DANCY'S CATFISH FARM announced the wooden sign hung prominently above the cattle guard. It was a mute testimony to the owner's pride in the once prosperous business.

As Lauren drove the rental car through the gates, she sought to assure herself that she was prepared for the sight ahead. She quickly discovered that she wasn't. The devastation was more overwhelming when viewed in person.

As far as the eye could see, the ground was coated with thick black crude oil. The biting stench filled the air, making Lauren fumble through her purse for a handkerchief. She climbed from the car slowly, covering her nose with the cloth.

The EPA was on the scene, overseeing the recovery process. A fine, based upon the amount of oil released, would be levied on the pipeline. Lauren knew that with the size of the line and at the rate it was pumping, as many as three or four hundred barrels could have been dispersed even in the short length of time before they'd shut down number four.

The whine of the dozers and heavy earth-moving equipment was deafening as they plowed to build dikes to contain the spill. Men shouted back and forth, adding more clamor to the chaos. Vandis Pipelines was working to recover as much as possible, but in this case if the spill was too large, they would have to haul the soil away in trucks to a toxic dump sight before they could bring in fresh dirt.

Lauren was relieved to see that the small clapboard farmhouse looked untouched by the madness. Stepping onto the large, weathered porch, she took a moment to gather her wits. Drawing a fortifying breath, she pressed the doorbell.

For the first time in her life, Lauren knew what Daniel had felt like as he'd waited outside the lion's den.

When there was no answer, she pressed the bell again. Glancing at her watch, she saw that it was not quite ten o'clock. Maybe she had come too early, she thought. Her spirits soared. Perhaps Mr. Dancy hadn't been released from the hospital yet. A dismissal could take hours.

Yes, that must be it, she thought. Coyle Dancy hadn't been released from the hospital yet. She would have to come back later.

Feeling a rush of overwhelming relief, Lauren was turning away when she heard a familiar male voice shout, "Come in!"

Have mercy, she thought desperately. He *was* home, and his disposition didn't sound any sweeter than it had the day before.

Pushing the screen open a crack, Lauren hesitated until she heard another bellow. "Are you going to come in or not?"

Not, would be her first choice, but Lauren knew she'd come too far to back out now. With false bravado, she pushed the screen door open and entered.

"Mr. Dancy?"

"Yes?"

Lauren's eyes worked to adjust from the bright sunshine outdoors to the filtered light inside. "I was wondering if I might speak to you?"

"Sounds like you already are."

Crusty, Lauren thought, but she wasn't going to let him intimidate her. "Thank you."

Closing the screen carefully, she walked to the center of the room and paused as she tried to focus on her surroundings.

The room seemed large and comfortable with its masculine furnishings. A massive fieldstone fireplace dominated the entire north wall. Grouped in clusters were cream-colored sofas and cushiony, overstuffed chairs in blue and cream plaid. The furniture was worn, but still acceptable to the eye.

Dappled sunlight from a series of windows on the east side cast a cheery glow on the polished hardwood beneath handwoven rugs. A faint smell of lemon polish drifted pleasantly from the oak tables. The atmosphere seemed to offer a pleasant sense of ease.

Despite whoever—or whatever—Coyle Dancy was, he had good taste.

"Are you a nurse?"

The crisp inquiry brought Lauren back to the present.

"Yes, I am." Her smile was honest, and so was her answer. Or I was until a few months ago, she amended silently, wondering what it was about her that made her former profession obvious to a complete stranger.

Her puzzled gaze finally located his voice. The man was lying in a hospital bed in a small alcove off to the left.

Like the rest of the room, the alcove looked bright and cheerful, surrounded by windows draped with freshly laundered blue Cape Cod curtains. The man's leg, encased in a heavy cast, was carefully propped on several pillows, a sight Lauren had expected.

What she hadn't expected was the man himself.

Coyle Dancy was certainly not elderly, nor did he give the appearance of being forbidding.

Lauren judged him to be close to her own age, maybe a few years older. He was handsome in a rugged sort of way, although it was hard for her to tell in his pitiful condition.

Dark, angry bruises mingled with a row of long stitches along his left brow. The right side of his face was covered with cuts and scratches, and his right eye was swollen completely shut. One leg was in a plaster cast from his ankle to his hip. His chest, which was as broad as Texas, was swathed tightly in layers of bandages to protect his broken ribs.

Still, an air of magnetism and raw masculinity surrounded his boyish head of wavy black hair. His blue eyes were electrifying.

Even in his present condition, it was easy for Lauren to see why women in Picayune found Coyle Dancy so charming.

"Have a seat," he invited.

"Thank you." Lauren edged toward the chair next to the bed and seated herself.

Ignoring her for the moment, Coyle stretched toward a table for a glass of water and swore under his breath when the pitcher proved to be out of his reach.

"Please, allow me." Lauren stood and quickly filled the glass with water and handed it to him.

"Thanks. This cast makes me almost helpless," he conceded in a disgruntled tone.

"I'm sure you must be miserable." Lauren automatically fluffed the flattened pillows and straightened the sheet before sitting down again.

"Does it look like rain?" he asked apprehensively.

"I hadn't noticed."

"The weatherman's predicting rain by nightfall," Coyle remarked, and Lauren noted more than a hint of disgust in his voice. "That's all I need—a gully washer to carry that oil to every river within a fifty-mile radius."

"Oh, I'm sure that won't happen," Lauren said consolingly. "The sun's shining now. If the rain holds off for another couple of hours, the workers should have the pipe repaired. Then they can begin to effectively contain the seepage."

Ordinarily, it took only a few hours to repair a ruptured pipeline, but because of the sheer magnitude of the eruption and because the pipes were so old, it was taking longer.

"I don't know . . . I'm sorry. I didn't catch your name." With a vague uneasiness, Coyle turned his full attention to the attractive blonde with smoke-gray eyes and thick, dark lashes.

True, he hadn't specifically asked the nurses' registry to send an older woman; he'd just assumed that they would. He wasn't sure he'd be comfortable with a nurse so close to his own age—or one so well built.

Without a doubt, she would be able to make his convalescence more pleasant, but Coyle wasn't looking for diversion. All he wanted was good nursing care until he was back on his feet and able to take care of himself again.

"Yes . . . I'm sorry." Lauren took a deep breath and braced herself for the explosion she felt certain would come when she introduced herself. "My name is Lauren—"

The phone rang.

Lauren nearly fainted with relief before she glanced at Coyle expectantly. "Would you like for me to answer that?"

"No, I can." Lauren watched Coyle pick up a wire coat hanger that had been straightened on one end and bent on the other. He looped one end of the wire over the phone. With one efficient jerk, the receiver was lying within easy grasp on his bed. Coyle grinned lopsidedly as he watched first disbelief, then admiration cross her face. "I thought I'd probably have to practice this more to get good at it," he confided with what Lauren thought was a shameless lack of modesty.

He scooped up the receiver. "Dancy, here."

Lauren watched as a stormy look crossed his face. "Yeah, Lenny, what'd you find out?"

Coyle listened a moment and responded sharply, "Vandis Pipelines, huh?"

Lauren unconsciously sat up straighter.

"Well, you're the lawyer. What do we do first?" Coyle demanded.

Lauren wished she could hear the other end of the conversation, but on second thought she was glad she couldn't. She had a sinking feeling that it would make what she'd come to do much harder.

"That's right—the pipe was *not* marked. I'm sure of it! . . . I don't know, Lenny. That's your job. Just make sure those idiots know they've not only killed all my catfish stock, they killed my two bird dogs and a dozen walnut trees that were over a hundred years old!"

Lauren's stomach churned. His prized dogs were dead, and he'd lost hundred-year-old walnut trees—the disaster was getting worse by the moment.

"Of course I want punitive damages! I want those people to compensate me for pain and suffering, mental anguish, loss of property . . ."

Lauren winced as the list raged on. Even if she *had* paid the insurance payment, Vandis Pipelines would still be in a world of trouble, she thought miserably.

When Coyle finished his conversation and handed the receiver to Lauren to hang up, she tried to summon a brave smile.

"Miserable half-wits . . . now where were we?"

Lauren swallowed. "We were about to introduce ourselves."

"I'm Coyle Dancy," he said, disinterested in her identity for the time being. "The job is simple. The doc said I could recuperate at home, but I'll need someone to take care of me. I have a housekeeper who comes in twice a week, so you wouldn't have to do anything except see to my meals and . . . whatever you nurses do in the way of baths and . . ." Coyle's voice trailed off, and he looked her over again uneasily. She was too attractive. . . . "Maybe you'd like to think this over?"

Lauren returned his look blankly. Was he assuming that she was from a nurses' registry? "Uh, no . . . you see, I'm not here—"

"Well, suit yourself," Coyle conceded. He'd never been good at this sort of thing. Just because she was pretty was no reason to deny her the position, Coyle reasoned, trying to be as impartial as he could. For all he knew, she might need the work, and she seemed to have a pleasant personality.

The wheels in Lauren's mind began to turn as she realized his mistake. Dare she attempt to go along with his misconception? If she did, it would present a possibility she hadn't expected. She sat up straighter. Why not? She *could* pose as his nurse, she mused, as she began to flirt dangerously with the idea. If she could get away with the deception for a day or two, she might be able to win Dancy's confidence before admitting who she really was. . . . Her imagination came to a skidding halt. Don't *even* think it, Lauren, she warned herself sternly. Not only would it be insane, but you could never pull it off.

"I'm afraid you misunderstood, Mr. Dancy."

"Misunderstood what?"

"I'm here . . ." Lauren swallowed, then drew in a deep breath. "You see, I . . ."

Coyle could sense that she, too, had reservations about nursing a man so close to her own age. Coyle had assumed that it wouldn't bother a professional, but he could see that it did, so he would try to let her off the hook discreetly.

"Well, if you need to think about it, I can interview a few others. . . ."

"That isn't it. . . ." Spit it out, Lauren, she told herself. Tell him who you are, make your apologies, and get the devil out of here!

Suddenly a loud blast shattered the stillness of the small farmhouse as the cleanup crew exploded dynamite to contain the spill.

"Those miserable weasels! I'm going to make Vandis Pipelines pay through the nose for this!" Coyle vowed as the house reverberated with another thunderous boom. "If I could get my hands on just one of the miserable blockheads responsible for this, I'd . . . I'd . . . ."

Lauren watched wide-eyed as Coyle's face flushed crimson as he searched for a word strong enough to describe what he'd do to the ones responsible for such an incomprehensible act of negligence. "Idiots! They're nothing but idiots!"

Lauren winced and inquired in a small voice, "Are you sure it's the pipeline's fault?"

Coyle's one good eye regarded her as if she'd lost her mind. "What?"

Realizing he wasn't in the mood to be impartial, Lauren tried to temper her impetuous question. "What I mean is . . . has it been determined yet exactly which party was at fault?"

To Lauren, Coyle seemed totally unfair. If the pipeline had been marked, which Cooper thought it had, then Coyle Dancy was at fault for the rupture, not Vandis Pipelines. But she could see by the stunned expression on Coyle's face that he'd never considered that possibility.

"I *know* who's at fault. Vandis Pipelines is guilty," Coyle stated unequivocally. "And they are going to pay, Ms. . . ." The finger he'd been shaking paused in midair. "What did you say your name was?"

"Lauren."

"Lauren what?"

Tell him, screamed her conscience silently. She had to quit being such a coward. He could only order her out of his house, a request that, at this point, she'd be happy to honor.

"Lauren Van . . . derpool." She smiled lamely. "Lauren Vanderpool . . . R.N." The words were out of Lauren's mouth before she realized what she was saying.

Coyle suddenly returned the smile, and Lauren felt her resolve weaken further. "Look . . ." His smile turned into a lopsided grin, a totally appealing male expression designed to charm a woman, and it was working amazingly well on Lauren. "I'm sorry for shouting, Lauren. I shouldn't be taking my frustrations out on you. After all, you're not the guilty party. I hope you'll forgive my lack of manners."

Lauren found it impossible to correct him. All traces of his earlier unpleasantness had disappeared, and now she was confronted with a man who was obviously in pain, a man who had every right to be mad at the world, a man who was humbly apologizing to her—of all people—for his lack of congeniality.

Lauren felt like dirt.

"There's no need to apologize, Mr. Dancy. If the pipeline was at fault, you may rest assured that you'll be treated fairly." Her words came out sounding more contrite than she'd intended.

Coyle gazed back at her oddly. "Oh?"

She averted his eyes, praying he wouldn't try to delve into the reason for her remark.

"You can bet your sweet life they'll treat me fairly," he said before returning to the subject at hand. "Well, how about it, Ms. Vanderpool. Do you want the job?"

Now was her moment of reckoning. She could either tell him the truth about who she was and face his unavoidable wrath or she could accept the nursing position he was offering and hope to continue the deception for a few days.

If she continued to deceive him, she knew it could backfire and make an already impossible situation even worse.

Could she get away with it? she wondered. She wasn't sure, but she suddenly decided she was going to try.

"Exactly what does the job entail, Mr. Dancy?" she asked, stalling.

"As I mentioned—general nursing duties and alternating meal preparation with my housekeeper for the next six to eight weeks. You'll have room and board in addition to your usual wage, and at times when I don't require your help, you'll be free to attend to your personal matters. Are you married, Ms. Vanderpool?"

"No."

"About to be?" he inquired casually.

"No, I have no commitments."

"Good. Then we should get along fine." He flashed her another congenial smile. "You may take the room closest to the kitchen—I think you'll find everything you need. I assume if you take the position that you'll be free to start right away?"

"If that's what you want. I'll have to leave to gather some things." Lauren rose on shaky knees. She couldn't believe she was doing this. How would she explain this blatant lie to him when the truth finally came out?

How would she explain to Cooper and Burke Hunter that she'd taken a job as Coyle Dancy's nurse?

And yet it seemed to her that she'd gone too far to back out now. Her only choice was to win Dancy's respect, and the only way to win that respect was to be around him. "Is there anything you need before I leave?" Lauren asked politely.

"I'll be fine till you get back." Coyle extended his hand to her. She grasped it, and they sealed the deal.

"I'm not big on roast," he warned.

Lauren's brows lifted. "Roast?"

"I'm trying to cut down on red meat. Stick to chicken and fish when you plan the menus."

"I will."

"How long do you think you'll be gone?"

"Less than an hour." It wouldn't take long for Lauren to return to the motel and retrieve her overnight bag.

Her mind still raced with unanswered questions. What would she do for clothes? She'd brought only a pair of pajamas and a toothbrush. Could she invent a plausible excuse for Cooper that wouldn't arouse his suspicions when she asked him to send her enough clothing to last three or four days?

She assumed she'd be safe there. Her father would never in a thousand years guess what she was up to.

Even she didn't believe what she was doing.

And what about the nursing service Coyle Dancy had called? Lauren would have to somehow find out the name and call immediately to tell them the position had been filled, or he'd discover she was an impostor.

"If you don't mind, hand me my medication

before you leave," Coyle requested. "I think I'll take it so I can sleep until you get back."

"Of course." Lauren reached for the assortment of brown bottles sitting on the table beside his bed and read each label. Removing a tablet from one bottle, she poured a fresh glass of water and dropped the pill into his waiting palm.

"Anything else?"

"No, thanks." Coyle leaned back onto the fold of the pillow and sighed. "It's going to be a long eight weeks, Ms. Vanderpool. I'm not used to lying in bed."

"We'll try to make your confinement pass as quickly as possible," Lauren promised. She tucked the sheet closer around him, trying to ignore his hair-covered chest, which was bare with the exception of the bandages. "I should be back within the hour."

"Sounds good." The phone rang again, and Lauren reached to answer it.

"You run along, Ms. Vanderpool. It's probably Petersen's calling to see if I've made a decision yet. I'll let them know the position's been filled." Coyle reached for the coat hanger as Lauren walked to the door.

Petersen's? Had fate just been kind enough to solve at least one of her problems? The moment she returned to the motel, she would check the phone book for a listing for Petersen's medical or nursing service. She prayed there would be one and that she could come up with a good enough excuse to satisfy the owner as to why Coyle Dancy had hired someone other than their applicants.

"Should I stop by the market for groceries?"

"The refrigerator has enough in it to last us through a famine."

After he'd gotten home this morning, Coyle had found that thoughtful friends and neighbors had cleaned his house and overstocked his refrigerator.

The phone rang again as Lauren slipped out the door.

"Hello."

"Mr. Dancy?"

"Yes?"

"This is Madelyn Garrett with Petersen's Medical Services."

"I thought it might be you."

"I just wanted to let you know it looks like it'll be late afternoon before we can send someone out. Will this be inconvenient for you?"

Coyle's gaze snapped back to the door Lauren had just exited. "What?"

Madelyn repeated her apologies. "We have a woman who's willing to accept the position, but she isn't able to start until late this afternoon. I'm calling to make sure you'll be able to manage until she gets there."

Coyle was confused. "Are you sure?"

"About what, Mr. Dancy?"

"About what time the woman said she'd get here." Undoubtedly Lauren Vanderpool had neglected to call the nursing service to tell them she'd arrive earlier, Coyle reasoned.

"Yes . . . Mavis McCord is one of our most qualified nurses, Mr. Dancy, and, after you've met her, I'm sure you'll agree that the wait was worth the inconvenience."

"Mavis McCord?" Coyle repeated vacuously. He was becoming more confused by the moment.

"Yes."

"Are you sure her name isn't Lauren Vanderpool?"

"Vanderpool?" Now Madelyn sounded confused. Coyle could hear her rifling through papers, rechecking her information. "We don't have a Lauren Vanderpool registered with us. Mavis McCord is the nurse we have scheduled to attend you."

"Well I'll be. . . ." Coyle's eyes narrowed as he surveyed the empty doorway again. Who in the devil was Lauren Vanderpool, and why had she lied to get the job? "Listen, Ms. Garrett. I think there's been some sort of mix-up," Coyle said. "Why don't you hold off on sending Mavis out here until I get back in touch with you."

"Are you sure, Mr. Dancy? Mavis will be able to come shortly after four. She's an excellent nurse."

"I'm sure she is, Ms. Garrett, but I might not be needing someone after all."

"Oh?"

"There was a woman here earlier wanting the job. I suppose the hospital sent her. Anyway, let me check it out and get back with you."

"Certainly, Mr. Dancy. I'll be waiting to hear from you if you change your mind."

"Sure . . . I'll let you know."

Coyle grunted as he leaned to replace the phone on the hook. A fine sheen of perspiration broke out across his forehead from the excruciating pain caused by the slight movement. Collapsing against the pillow, Coyle gazed at the ceiling for a moment, trying to figure out what could be going on.

Who was Lauren Vanderpool?

Madelyn Garrett had said she wasn't associated with Petersen's Medical Services.

Coyle managed to retrieve the phone and dial the hospital. Minutes later he hung up thoughtfully. The hospital had never heard of Lauren Vanderpool.

He lay for another five minutes, mulling over the strange situation. Now, who would want to come into his house to pass herself off as a nurse?

For the life of him, Coyle couldn't think of anyone who would have a reason to do that. . . . Unless . . . His face suddenly puckered. Oh those *rotten* bloodsuckers! Did they think he was born yesterday?

Hooking the receiver again, Coyle dialed his lawyer's office with short, angry punches.

"Janie, let me speak to Lenny," Coyle snapped, and a few seconds later his attorney came on the line.

"Lenny. Coyle. I want you to check out something for me."

"What is it?" Lenny asked.

"Find out if anyone connected with Vandis Pipelines has a daughter named Lauren," Coyle demanded in a tight voice. "And get back to me as soon as you can."

Chapter Four

❖ ❖ ❖

HER ACTIONS WERE not only rash they were foolish, Lauren told herself beratingly on the drive back to the motel. She won't be able to get away with this for more than a day or two at the most. How could she do anything so irresponsible?

But on the other hand, she argued, accepting the position as Coyle Dancy's nurse didn't necessarily mean she'd made matters worse. She was a competent nurse, so she wouldn't be jeopardizing Coyle's health. Accepting the job didn't seem unethical to her because she planned to do everything she could to make his injuries more tolerable.

In the long run the misrepresentation might even turn out to be a wise decision. Any moment the insurance company would notify Cooper that his policy had lapsed.

A shudder rippled through Lauren at the grim thought. When that occurred, it would make it easier to explain to Cooper why she was making this desperate attempt to win Coyle Dancy's approval before she revealed her true purpose and identity.

Lauren didn't try to kid herself that once Dancy found out who she was he would be benevolent about the deception, but she still hoped he would show a modicum of common sense when he learned the truth.

He'd be livid, but Lauren sensed that in spite of all his blustering, Coyle could be a reasonable man, and a reasonable man should know that he couldn't squeeze blood out of a turnip.

With any luck at all, by the time he discovered who she was, it would have already been decided that he was the party at fault.

Lauren concluded that in the unlikely event the pipeline turned out to be at fault and Dancy hoped to be compensated for his losses, then, despite her deception, he'd have no other choice but to calm down and negotiate for a just settlement.

At least that's the way Lauren hoped it would work as she stopped in front of the motel.

All she needed was a little time to win Coyle Dancy's confidence, time to prove to him that even though she'd deliberately misled him in a moment of temporary insanity, she'd had no intent to defraud him.

Entering the motel room, Lauren's eyes were immediately drawn to the message light flashing on the telephone beside the bed. She quickly picked up the receiver and dialed the motel operator, reasoning that since Cooper was the only one who knew where she was, the message would be from him.

To Lauren's surprise, the message was not from her father. It was from Gloria Richland, a woman Cooper had been dating for the past couple of years.

The clerk gave Lauren a phone number and quoted the message, "Lauren, please return my call the moment you get in. Gloria."

Puzzled, Lauren thanked her and hung up. She sat for a moment looking at the number she'd scribbled down. It wasn't familiar, nor did the brief message lend a clue as to why Gloria had called.

Lauren lifted the receiver and dialed the number. She waited as the phone rang five times before a man answered. "Hello."

"My name is Lauren Vandis. I received a message that Gloria Richland could be reached at this number."

"Hold on a minute, I'll check."

Lauren listened as the man cupped his hand over the mouthpiece and asked in a raised voice, "Anyone in here by the name of Richland?"

Moments later a woman came on the line. "Yes?"

"Gloria, this is Lauren."

"Oh, Lauren, thank God."

Lauren heard Gloria's sigh and felt a shiver of dread. "I got your message, Gloria. . . . Is anything wrong?"

"Lauren, Cooper had another heart attack around seven this morning."

Fearing the worst, Lauren sank onto the bed and closed her eyes. "How bad is it, Gloria?"

"I'm not sure. He's in intensive care—the doctors are still with him. I don't know how bad it is this time, Lauren. . . ." Gloria's voice broke with emotion. She had been with Cooper during his last heart attack and had thought she'd lost him then.

"I'll take the next plane out."

"Wait a minute, Lauren. Dr. Franks is coming out of Cooper's room now."

Dr. Theodore Franks had seen Cooper through kidney stones, gallbladder surgery, and two previous heart attacks. Lauren knew her father couldn't be in better hands, yet she dreaded the prognosis. Lauren waited tensely while Gloria exchanged a few words with the doctor before putting him on the line.

"Lauren?" The doctor sounded tired and very far away.

"Yes."

"Well, it looks like we lucked out again."

Lauren's shoulders sagged with relief. "Is Dad all right?"

"He's not all right, but he's stable, and it looks like the crisis is over for the time being. I'll keep him in intensive care for a few days. Then I'll see if I can't persuade him to throw away the cigarettes and change his diet."

"I'm sorry . . . I've tried, but he's so—"

"You don't need to tell me about Cooper," Ted interjected. "He has ignored my advice for thirty years. It's a good thing he's strong as a bull moose, but I'll warn him again that if he doesn't make up his mind to change his life-style, his luck will run out one of these days."

"I'll fly home immediately," Lauren promised. "Where are you?"

"I'm in Mississippi, taking care of some business for Dad."

"Does it concern the pipeline rupture?"

"Yes." Lauren had no idea what to do about Coyle Dancy. He was expecting her to return within the hour, but she knew if Cooper needed her, she had no choice but to return to Shreveport immediately.

Ted sighed. "That's all Cooper's been talking about. He said to assure you that he's okay. He insists that you go ahead and finish your business before you fly back to Louisiana."

"Shouldn't I be with Dad?"

"There's not much you can do," Ted admitted. "Gloria's standing by. If any complications develop, she'll contact you. I think Cooper might rest better if he knew you were taking care of matters, Lauren. He's pretty upset about the spill."

"Do you think that's what brought on this attack?"

"It might have helped, but as you know, there were other contributing factors."

She knew only too well. A new, even more disturbing thought crossed her mind. "Dad hasn't heard from the insurance company, has he?"

"Insurance? I don't know—he didn't mention anything about it. Was he supposed to?"

"It's probably too soon," Lauren admitted in a preoccupied tone.

"Take care of yourself, Lauren. Here's Gloria."

"Lauren?" Gloria prompted a second later.

"Yes?"

"I think what Dr. Franks advised would be best," Gloria confided. "Cooper's worried sick about the spill, and he's very anxious for you to report back to him."

"Actually I haven't got anything to report, Gloria. I'm afraid things are moving slowly on this end."

"Have you spoken with Mr. Dancy yet?"

"Briefly." Lauren didn't want to lie to Gloria, but Cooper's condition made it impossible for her to explain what she'd done. "I'm supposed to see him later this afternoon."

"Good. Cooper will want to know the minute you talk to him."

"Gloria . . . are you sure you don't need me there?"

"You take care of things on that end. Cooper wants you and Burke to make sure everything is going smoothly in his absence."

Burke. Lauren felt ill at the thought of having

to confront the company lawyer with what she'd done. "What time is Burke due back?"

"I'm not sure. I think it'll be sometime late this evening. I'll have him call you the moment he gets here."

"Gloria . . . I'm going to be changing locations." Lauren broached the subject carefully. If Cooper didn't need her, she planned to carry out what she'd started, no matter how crazy it was. She was committed, and she saw no other way but to follow through. "The place I'm staying now isn't comfortable," Lauren explained, "plus, it's a long drive to the Dancy farm. I'm going to move closer."

"Oh?" Gloria sounded puzzled.

"I'm not sure where I'll be, but I'll let you know when I'm settled again." Lauren hated having to tell another lie to cover the last one.

"You mean I won't have a number where I can reach you?" Gloria sounded surprised and concerned that she wouldn't be able to reach Lauren in case there was a change in Cooper's condition.

"I'll phone you at least twice a day," Lauren promised. "If Dad continues to progress well, it's possible I may need to stay here a few more days, Gloria. It won't be easy. Mr. Dancy is understandably upset about the accident."

"I'm sure he is." Gloria's tone was sympathetic, which made Lauren feel even worse about her lying. "Are you okay?" Gloria asked.

"I'm fine. Just take good care of Dad until I get back home."

"I will . . . but what about Burke? I'm sure he'll want to talk to you the moment he arrives in Shreveport."

"I'll keep in touch," Lauren promised. She didn't know how she'd manage it since she'd be living in Coyle Dancy's home, but she'd have to find a way. "Oh . . . Gloria, I'm going to need some extra clothing. Could you stop by my apartment and pack a few things to send to me?"

"Of course. What do you need?"

"Enough clothing and lingerie to last a few days. You know jeans, blouses, and a couple of skirts. Since I'm not sure where I'll be staying, just send a bag to the airport and I'll pick it up there."

"All right. Cooper has a key to your apartment, doesn't he?"

"Yes . . . and Gloria, tell Dad not to worry. I love him. Assure him that I'll take care of everything."

As Lauren hung up, she was even more convinced that she had no choice but to continue the charade.

If she flew home and left Dancy high and dry, he would be even angrier when he found out who she was. But if she stayed, even for a day, she just might be able to pull this thing off.

She glanced at the telephone book and remembered that she still had to inform the nursing service that the position with Coyle Dancy had been filled.

Thumbing through the yellow pages, Lauren scanned the columns, holding her breath until she located the number for Petersen's. She dialed and waited.

"Petersen's Medical Services," announced a pleasant voice.

"I'm calling on behalf of Coyle Dancy."

Madelyn Garrett cleared her throat. "Does Mr. Dancy want me to send Mavis?"

Mavis? Who was Mavis? Lauren thought frantically as she racked her brain for a sensible answer. "No, he wants me to inform you that the nursing position he requested has been filled."

"Oh?" Disappointment was evident in Madelyn's voice, but she remained cordial. "I'll call Mrs. McCord and tell her not to make the trip. I know she'll be disappointed that she didn't get this assignment."

"If things don't work out, Mr. Dancy will be back in touch with you in a couple of days," Lauren promised, feeling better about her deception because she knew that this woman would be hearing from Coyle Dancy sooner than she imagined.

"Tell Mr. Dancy that I hope we didn't inconvenience him by not having someone available earlier. I just know he would have loved Mavis."

"I'll tell him."

As Lauren hung up and reached for her overnight case, she was determined to overcome the odds that had led her to deceive so many. She would bluff her way through this if it killed her.

"What was the name of that chicken dish?" Coyle lay back on the pillows and watched Lauren refill his empty coffee cup.

The evening meal had been delicious, one of the best Coyle had ever eaten. Whoever this attractive impostor was, she could cook.

"I don't think it has a name. My mother used to fix it twice a week. It's just vegetables and chicken in a sauce." Lauren smiled. "I'm glad you enjoyed it."

It had been so late in the afternoon when Lauren had returned to the Dancy farm that she'd barely had time to deposit her overnight bag in her room before starting dinner.

Her bedroom had looked clean and comfortable with a white chenille spread on the double bed and freshly laundered Priscilla curtains ruffling in the breeze from the open window.

"It was good," Coyle complimented her again. "You're an excellent cook, Lauren . . . Vanderpool, is it?"

Coyle waited until Lauren's eyes met his.

"Yes," she answered quietly.

Lauren hurriedly picked up his empty dinner tray and started for the kitchen. Coyle was making her nervous. He'd watched every move she'd made all evening with what Lauren would term a critical eye.

Perhaps, she reasoned, he was only trying to decide whether she was competent, or was he already beginning to suspect something?

Lauren decided it was just her guilty conscience tormenting her. If Coyle suspected something, he'd make no bones about confronting her with it.

In the few hours since she'd met him, it was clear to Lauren that Coyle Dancy was not the sort of man to play games.

If he'd suspected she was anyone other than who she said she was, she'd be out the front door on her ear faster than she cared to think about.

"Yes, what?" Coyle countered dryly.

He'd watched her closely, and she was as nervous as a long-tailed cat in a room full of rocking chairs. Yet she'd given him no clues as to her real identity. Whoever she was, Coyle had to admit she was playing it cool. But then, so was he.

"Lauren Vanderpool?" he repeated.

Lauren paused, keeping her back to him as she answered his inquiry. "Yes, my name is Lauren. Would you care for anything else?"

"Not now." Coyle reached for a dinner mint lying on the table beside his bed. "You from around here?"

"No."

"Close by?"

"Not really." She was deliberately being evasive, and he knew it. "I'll be in the kitchen if you need anything," Lauren announced.

"Okay."

After Lauren had left the room, Coyle unwrapped the mint slowly and lay back on his pillow, thinking about the stranger in his house.

She'd insisted her name was "Lauren." Coyle could almost buy that part of the deception by the sincerity in her voice. But he'd noticed that she hadn't sounded quite so convincing about her last name.

Then who was she? The question had nagged him all afternoon. Was it possible she was from the pipeline company? Had the big shots sent a pretty face to smooth matters over until their lawyers took over?

Coyle took a bite of the candy thoughtfully. Lauren Vanderpool, or whoever she was, was good-looking all right, and she didn't seem dumb.

Ordinarily Coyle wasn't attracted to blondes, but this one looked like she wasn't all fluff and artificial glamour.

Her makeup looked the way Coyle liked, light

enough so that it didn't conceal her flawless complexion, yet enough to give her a healthy glow.

This woman had a way of meeting his gaze with her serious, wide-set gray eyes that gave nothing away but made a man wonder exactly what lay in their mysterious depths.

The owners of the pipeline would be crazy if they thought they could send a woman to try to placate him, Coyle mused, and yet, if they panicked, they might be foolish enough to try to pull one over on him. Would they be that desperate? he wondered. The pipeline would undoubtedly have enough insurance to cover their loss, so why would they risk raising his ire with such a foolish ploy?

It didn't make sense to him. But why else would a woman waltz in and pass herself off as a nurse if there wasn't something sneaky and underhanded going on?

The phone rang, and Coyle used his bent coat hanger to snare the receiver.

"Coyle. Lenny."

"What'd you find out?"

"We hit pay dirt."

Coyle glanced at the doorway that led into the kitchen. He could hear Lauren moving about as she stacked dishes in the dishwasher. "Give it to me."

"Vandis Pipelines is owned by Cooper Vandis.

Cooper Vandis does have a daughter by the name of Lauren. How did you know that?"

"Lucky guess." Lauren Vandis . . . Lauren Vanderpool. Coyle shook his head in disbelief. The fools.

"The daughter is blonde, gray eyes—"

"Five foot four or five," Coyle interrupted, "weighing around a hundred and twenty pounds. She's twenty-eight or twenty-nine years old and good-looking," Coyle finished for him.

"Bingo. It seems she and her father run the pipeline."

"No kidding." Of all the nerve! And she was going to try to pass herself off as a nurse and take care of him!

"Coyle, what's going on out there?" Lenny demanded.

"Cooper Vandis has apparently sent his daughter down here to pull a fast one on us, Lenny."

For a moment Lenny seemed to find the news hard to digest. "You must be kidding."

"No, I'm not. Unless I miss my guess, Lauren Vandis showed up on my doorstep this morning and passed herself off as a nurse."

"And you hired her?"

"I didn't know who she was then! I have a broken leg, two busted ribs, and every bone in my body aches. Of course I hired her."

Lenny let out a low whistle. "They're either crazy or extremely desperate."

"That's what I'm thinking. Have you talked to anyone about the pipeline's insurance coverage?"

"I spoke to one of the adjusters this afternoon. There doesn't appear to be a problem."

Coyle shook his head again. "Then what is Cooper Vandis trying to pull?"

"I wouldn't have the slightest idea, but whatever it is, we don't want any part of it. Get rid of her."

"I plan to, just as soon as I give her enough rope to hang herself, then I'm going to tell her where she and the pipeline can stick their unamusing little charade."

"No good, Coyle. You'd better nip this in the bud right now," Lenny warned. "Make it clear that you know who she is and send her packing. We have a meeting with their lawyer sometime late tomorrow afternoon. I'll voice my strong objection to their tactics, and I'll warn him not to try anything like this again. Now get rid of her, Coyle. Tonight."

Coyle's eyes narrowed as they focused on the doorway to the kitchen. There was no way he was going to let that little schemer off the hook so easily. "I said I would, Lenny. I'm just going to have a little fun before I do."

"Come on, Coyle. I know you. You're bored and irritated. Don't make matters worse by making a game out of this. We've got the upper hand; let's keep it that way."

75

"I'll get rid of her . . . first thing tomorrow morning," Coyle promised. "I have to go now, Lenny. She's coming back."

"Coyle!"

Coyle severed the connection as Lenny continued to voice his protest.

Lauren walked into the room as Coyle struggled to hang up the receiver. "Please, allow me," she said, taking the receiver and placing it on the hook efficiently. "Will there be anything else, Mr. Dancy?"

Coyle smiled. "Why don't you call me Coyle."

"If you'll call me Lauren."

I certainly will, Coyle thought as he nodded, about five seconds before I call you a cab.

"If there's nothing else you need, I think I'll get settled in my room." Lauren brought her hand up to her mouth to conceal a tired yawn. She still had to phone the hospital to check on Cooper's condition. She was looking forward to a hot bath and a good night's sleep before she faced the lion in his den the next morning.

"I don't need anything," Coyle declared. "Oh, except you might readjust my pillows."

"Certainly." Lauren stepped forward, and Coyle made an effort to sit up. She heard him groan as he grasped his side.

"I'm sorry . . . are you in pain?"

"A little."

"Is it time for more medication?" Lauren

reached for one of the vials containing a pain reliever.

Coyle drew back defensively. He wasn't about to let someone who worked at a pipeline administer his medication, even if the instructions were clearly printed on the labels. "I don't need it yet."

"Is your side hurting?"

"I think it's my back. It feels like something's sticking me."

Ignoring his objection, Lauren poured a glass of water and shook two pills into his hand. He eyed them distrustfully for a moment, then grudgingly swallowed the medicine.

"My back still hurts."

"Let me see." Lauren felt shy as she leaned closer to check his discomfort.

Bare-chested men had never bothered her before, but for some reason this bare-chested man made her feel slightly giddy.

"I don't see anything." She ran her hand over the smooth, tanned expanse of his back, reminding herself that she shouldn't be enjoying what was a strictly professional procedure. But this man was a prize specimen.

Her hand smoothing across his skin made Coyle tense. He reminded himself he'd have to be careful or this could backfire on him. Her touch was light and businesslike, but still it brought a warmth he found more pleasant than he'd expected. Of course, that's what Cooper Vandis was counting on, Coyle reminded himself, and that was exactly the last thing he was going to give him.

"Am I hurting you?" Lauren paused when she noticed Coyle looking at her strangely.

"No."

Her hand continued to massage and soothe. "There, does that feel better?"

The smell of her perfume drifted to Coyle as he tried to relax. She was too close, close enough to make him aware that she was all woman and that he hadn't shared a woman's company for a while.

He tensed again when her hand innocently brushed his arm as she leaned to adjust the light blanket. In spite of his injuries, a swift, almost painful desire rose to taunt him.

"Yeah, thanks. That's better."

Lauren straightened, surprised to discover that she was reluctant to break the contact. There was something about Coyle Dancy she was beginning to find intriguing. "Will that be all?"

Coyle eased himself away, but his blue eyes met and examined hers in a way that made her stomach jump with sudden expectation.

Coyle was adept at playing games with women. He knew exactly the right things to say at exactly the right times. He didn't enjoy playing games, but he could hold his own with the ones who did.

Apparently Lauren Vandis wanted to play nurse. Consequently Coyle Dancy was just ornery enough to indulge her whim.

"Ms. Vanderpool . . ." He flashed her a devastatingly boyish grin. "I mean, Lauren," he corrected subserviently.

"Yes?"

"I was thinking maybe a sponge bath might help me sleep better," Coyle confided in a voice that could only be described as suggestive.

Her gray eyes widened as he took her arm and pulled her slowly closer to him. "You wouldn't mind giving me one, would you . . . honey?"

Chapter Five

THE DOORBELL RANG before Lauren could think about what to do next, and the unexpected intrusion took both Lauren and Coyle by surprise.

"Who could that be?" Coyle grumbled as the bell sounded again.

Lauren moved away from the bed, thankful for the reprieve but puzzled by Coyle's abrupt change. She could feel his gaze following her as she walked across the room, and it made her feel jumpy. He'd called her "honey," a term Lauren didn't find strange coming from a man like Coyle Dancy, but until then he'd been a perfect gentleman. Why the sudden shift in attitude? she wondered.

Had he changed, or was her imagination working overtime again? She hoped it was the latter as she opened the door to see a lovely woman who had an even lovelier smile.

The woman seemed surprised to see Lauren, but she quickly recovered her composure, and her smile widened. "Hi. I know it's late, but if Coyle isn't sleeping, I'd like to see him."

"I've given him a sedative, but he's still awake." Lauren stepped back to allow the attractive brunette to enter. "May I say who is—"

"Elaine," Coyle interrupted, "what brings you out so late?"

"You, you big lug." Elaine handed Lauren a casserole dish still warm from the oven and started toward the alcove with a radiant smile on her face.

Lauren headed for the kitchen to deposit the casserole, discreetly ignoring the warm greeting Elaine placed on Coyle's mouth.

"You look terrible," Elaine empathized.

Coyle chuckled. "Thanks."

"I've wanted to call you all day, but I've been so rushed. Then I was afraid I might disturb you." Elaine pulled up a chair beside Coyle's bed and sat down as Lauren came back into the room.

Coyle's glance flickered coolly over Lauren before he turned his attention back to Elaine. "Did you work today?"

"I went to the office," Elaine said, "but the market is so glutted now that I practically have to get down on my hands and knees to beg the buyer to consider a piece of property."

"I guess it's tough everywhere."

Elaine glanced inquisitively at Lauren, then back to Coyle. "I'm surprised you located a nurse so soon. . . ."

"I was lucky," Coyle said before making a brisk introduction. "Lauren Vanderpool, Elaine Tarrasch."

Lauren returned Elaine's friendly smile.

Though Lauren didn't know what Elaine's relationship was with Coyle, she liked her instantly.

"Hello, Elaine."

"Hello, Lauren. Now, I want you to take good care of Coyle."

Lauren smiled. "I'll do my best."

Preliminary niceties completed, Elaine returned her attention to the patient. "How are you feeling today?"

"Sore."

"Oh, poor darling. Do you remember my being in the emergency room with you?"

"Barely . . . thanks for calling the truck lines for me." Coyle's grin was becoming appealingly drowsy. There was no longer any doubt in Lauren's mind that he and Elaine shared a deep affection for each other.

"You're most welcome. Jim said not to worry about your job. It will be waiting when you're able to return."

An uncharacteristic tug of envy tore at Lauren, and she was annoyed with herself. Why, she wondered with a touch of wistfulness, should it matter to her that Coyle Dancy was attracted to Elaine? Obviously Elaine was just the sort of woman who would attract a vibrant man like Coyle. Perhaps the envy she was feeling was because Lauren herself had never been that enthralled with a man.

Though she'd dated since she was sixteen, there had never been one special man in her life. Lauren found solace in the knowledge that she could have had steady relationships—many times—but by her own choice, she was still single at twenty-eight.

And not once over the years had she coveted the affection that another woman had received from a man, not until this moment, not until she'd met Coyle Dancy.

"Excuse me." Lauren hesitantly broke into the conversation, feeling uncomfortable as a third party. "May I fix you a cup of coffee, Elaine?"

"Why, yes, a cup of coffee would be nice. Thank you."

Lauren's eyes demurely met her employer's. "And you, Coyle?"

When Coyle returned Lauren's gaze almost insolently, she experienced the same unnerving apprehension she'd felt all evening.

"Sure, why not?" he said briskly. "Elaine might enjoy a piece of that chocolate cake Janine Miller brought by this afternoon," he added.

Lauren nodded and left the room as Elaine proceeded to share her day's events with Coyle.

As Lauren moved around the kitchen, she tried not to eavesdrop, but it was unavoidable. The kitchen didn't have a door she could close, so Lauren found herself inadvertently overhearing their visit.

"Do you know how bad your damages are yet?"

"I'm not sure, Elaine."

Lauren's trained ear noticed that Coyle's voice sounded tired. She decided she'd have to insist that Elaine keep her visit brief.

"I'm afraid they're extensive, though."

"It's such a shame," Elaine sympathized. "You could have been killed, Coyle!"

Lauren flinched at that.

"That's what they say."

She sliced two thick wedges of cake, thinking that surely Coyle must be weary of people reminding him of his close call. But if he was, he didn't show it.

"Well, I just hope that whoever is responsible for burying that pipeline and not marking it is going to pay for all your suffering," Elaine said heatedly.

There was a sharp flash of lightning, and a roll of thunder rumbled through the house.

Lauren leaned over the sink and lifted the kitchen curtain to peer out as the first drops of rain dotted the dusty windowpane. The thought of approaching rain made her as heartsick as she knew Coyle must feel. The workers had repaired the ruptured pipeline late that afternoon, but the ground was still saturated with crude oil. If rains washed the oil into nearby streams and wells, the cleanup would be more complicated.

Lauren let the curtain drop back into place.

Vandis Pipelines needed rain about as much as Coyle Dancy needed another broken leg.

"Mercy, it's humid." Elaine had picked up a magazine and began to fan herself as Lauren carried the tray of coffee and dessert into the alcove. "Coyle, you're going to have to replace that old air conditioner."

"I hope I don't anywhere near soon."

"The weatherman says we're in for a storm tonight. Maybe it'll break this terrible heat," Elaine said comfortingly.

A searing flash of lightning illuminated the room brightly, and another crack of thunder drowned the hum of the antiquated window air conditioner, which was laboring to cool the stagnant air.

Lauren placed the tray on a table and hurried to the window to look out anxiously. The black clouds churned ominously overhead as rain peppered down on the shingles.

"Oh, dear. It looks like the storm is about to break," Elaine fretted. She seemed to debate for a moment, then she reach for her purse. "I should be going before it sets in for the night."

"You don't need to hurry off," Coyle objected in a sleepy voice, but Elaine and Lauren could see that he was exhausted.

"I'll be back tomorrow," Elaine promised as she leaned over to kiss Coyle good-by. "You need your rest."

Lauren moved away from the window and busied herself with the untouched tray as the couple exchanged a few soft-spoken words. After a moment, Elaine straightened and turned to Lauren.

"It was nice meeting you, Lauren. I'm sure we'll be seeing each other often."

"I'm sure we will."

Elaine drew closer as Lauren walked her to the front door. "Take good care of him," she urged. "If you should need me, don't hesitate to call. Coyle has my number."

"Thank you, but I'm sure we'll be able to manage fine."

"Are you from around here?" Elaine asked, pausing at the door. She'd been trying to place Lauren. Most everyone knew everyone else in Picayune, and Elaine couldn't remember ever seeing Lauren before.

"I'm new to the area."

"Well, that explains it, I guess." Elaine frowned as another bolt of lightning brightened the doorway. "I knew I should have brought my umbrella."

A moment later, Lauren closed the door and switched off the porch light as the rain began to fall in a heavy downpour.

Leaning against the door frame, a feeling of loneliness suddenly washed over her. She hated what she was doing; she hated lies and deceit.

More than that, she hated lying to a decent person who might have been severely wronged. No matter who was at fault in the accident, Lauren realized that Coyle Dancy stood to lose the most.

Lauren knew she wanted to go home and see Cooper. . . . But more than that, Lauren discovered that she actually envied Elaine the friendship she shared with Coyle. The revelation was not only disconcerting, Lauren was mystified by it as well.

Coyle Dancy was a complete stranger to her, and yet Lauren felt a growing affinity for him that she was powerless to explain. It wasn't because he was a cranky, ruggedly handsome male, though Lauren had to admit Coyle had good reason to be cranky. If it weren't for his injuries, Coyle Dancy might even be a pleasant man to be around. But then, she wouldn't be around him once her business was concluded.

Shoving aside her melancholy thoughts, Lauren concluded that she must be overly tired. Tomorrow she would have everything back in perspective. She'd wrap up her business and be on her way back to Shreveport.

Coyle's eyes were closed as Lauren walked back into the alcove. Assuming that his sedative had taken effect, she began switching off lamps and preparing to retire to her room.

The approaching storm intensified. Bright

flashes of light darted eerily into corners of the dark room. Lauren moved quietly to Coyle's bedside and carefully adjusted the sheet over his chest. It occurred to her that it felt good to be doing something she loved again.

"Does it seem hot in here?" The sound of Coyle's voice startled her.

"It is stuffy," she acknowledged. Lauren knew the cast and bandages surrounding Coyle made the room seem warmer to him. "Are you uncomfortable?"

"I'm miserable."

She switched on the lamp beside the bed. "I'll check the controls on the air conditioner." Although, Lauren discovered, the unit was operating at full capacity, the room still felt like an oven.

Lauren eased the sheet down to the foot of the bed in an attempt to make the heat more bearable. It was no surprise to Lauren that the lower part of Coyle Dancy's body was as magnificent as his torso. Clad in a pair of blue briefs and a cast, Coyle would make any woman look twice. His legs were long and lean and covered in dark hair like his chest. Lauren figured the Lord must have had an exceptionally good day when he'd created Coyle Dancy.

"Is Elaine still here?" Coyle asked drowsily.

"She's gone."

"Elaine's okay." The room was once again

illuminated by a flash of lightning, followed by a thunderous boom.

"She seemed very pleasant." Lauren went about trying to ease Coyle's discomfort, preparing herself to hear how much in love he was with Elaine. "Have you known each other long?"

"A couple of years," Coyle murmured. "She's stood by me through thick and thin . . . ouch, take it easy."

Lauren stuck a thermometer into Coyle's mouth, annoyed with herself that his reply had bothered her. "Lie still, I'm going to get a basin of cool water," she ordered.

The medicine was beginning to take full effect. Coyle's muddled mind momentarily forgot his earlier plan to torment Lauren before announcing that he knew who she was and kicking her out. He forgot everything except the intense pain ravaging his body.

"Is it raining?" he asked after Lauren removed the thermometer. She frowned; his temperature was slightly elevated, but it was nothing unusual for a man with his injuries.

"Will your doctor be coming by in the morning?"

"I suppose I'm running a temperature."

Lauren smothered a smile at his fatalistic guess. She dipped a cloth into a basin of cool water and wrung it dry. "Why don't you relax and give the sedative a chance to work," she suggested gently.

The hands that softly worked the cloth across his feverish body were pliable, compassionate, and gentle—to Coyle, they seemed like the hands of an angel.

His torment began gradually to ease as Lauren sponged away the thin sheen of perspiration covering his lithe frame. A few minutes later the old window unit gave up the fight. It sputtered a few times and died.

"Maybe it blew a fuse." Coyle told Lauren where the fuse box was located, and she went to check.

Lauren returned with the grim observation that the problem was in the air conditioner itself. "I'll open a window."

Although the rain should have cooled the air, the storm had created so much humidity that Lauren thought she could slice it with a knife.

"There's a fan in my bedroom," Coyle suggested. "It isn't big, but it'll help."

Moments later Lauren plugged in the small fan, and the six-inch blade began to whirl, but it was too small to move enough air to do any good.

Lauren tried again to make Coyle as comfortable as possible under the conditions. The hour grew late as the medicine engulfed Coyle in its tranquilizing mist. After the sponge bath, Lauren gently rolled Coyle onto his side and began to massage his back. The thick ridge of muscles across his shoulder blades was taut with pain.

As she kneaded, Lauren spoke in easy tones, commenting on nothing of consequence. Lauren knew pain was more tolerable if the patient's mind was distracted.

Coyle struggled to remain conscious. While the rain beat a steady tattoo on the roof of the old farmhouse, he began gradually to relax.

"I don't think I'll be able to make it," he murmured.

Lauren assumed Coyle was concerned about his injuries. "You're doing fine," she said, hoping to allay his fear. "In a few days your body will begin to mend—"

"I'm not worried about my health; it's my farm. It's gone . . . all of it."

"You'll be able to rebuild," Lauren said soothingly. "As soon as you're back on your feet . . . and there's a settlement. . . ."

"Everything I owned I sank into this land." For the first time Lauren heard raw emotion in his voice. Anger and bitterness were gone, replaced by a deep hurt caused by the realization of what had happened. "This farm was my life, and even if I do get my money back, the land will be worthless for years. I'll have to start all over . . . and I'm not sure I can do it again."

"Shhhh. I'm sure that's how you feel now, but tomorrow you'll feel stronger . . . more capable of coping."

Coyle sighed. "For three long years I've worked day and night to build this place. I dug the ponds and raised the fry and fought disease and algae—all for nothing. The ponds will have to be restocked. My wells are polluted, which means I'll have to drill new ones. . . . I just won't have the stamina to go through it again."

"Have you always lived in Mississippi?" Lauren asked, hoping to steer his thoughts to a more pleasant subject.

"I used to live in L.A."

"In L.A.?" Lauren was surprised. "What did you do before you started farming?"

"Drove an eighteen-wheeler. I'm still forced to to make ends meet, but I hate every minute of it."

"Why?"

"I'm never home. I'm on the road every Thanksgiving and Christmas, and my dad's in poor health. When Mom died, my sister had to delay the funeral for three days because she couldn't find me. I don't want that to happen when I lose Dad."

"So you moved to Picayune, Mississippi and bought a catfish farm with hopes of a better life."

"I bought the land and then turned it into a catfish farm." Coyle's quiet voice filled with pride. "I've worked myself to death on this place. I worked the land by day and took half a year off to go to school at nights. I was finally getting close to the day that I was going to be able to quit driving the truck . . . but that will be impossible now."

"I'm so sorry," she murmured, "so very, very sorry."

"You have no idea of the problems a catfish farmer faces."

Lauren didn't, not the vaguest. In fact, she'd never cared for fish, and yesterday's events certainly hadn't changed her feelings about them.

"Proper water oxygen levels must be maintained in the ponds, or the fish will die," Coyle said. "The fish don't cooperate and grow to a uniform size. Then you have to contend with people sneaking in at night and stealing the food fish."

"Food fish?"

"Those are the fish that are ready to sell, some to bulk processing plants, some to live haulers, and the remainder go to feed lakes," Coyle explained. "And there's always the problem of keeping algae under control."

"I had no idea . . ."

"Most people don't."

"Excuse me, but if there are so many headaches, why do you even want to raise fish?" Lauren failed to see the attraction.

He sighed again. "In spite of all the problems, I love every minute of it. My farm was finally beginning to show real promise, until yesterday."

"I'm sure it will again." Lauren eased Coyle onto his back and tucked the sheet lightly around him. She was bone tired, but she knew she wouldn't rest until he was sleeping soundly.

It was too late to call the hospital to check on Cooper. Lauren prayed that there hadn't been any complications and that her father was resting comfortably.

She settled herself onto the chair beside the bed and listened to the rain. She was about to conclude that Coyle had finally drifted off when he asked, "What about you?"

"Me?"

"Tell me about you, Lauren Vanderpool." Coyle hadn't planned to bait her, but suddenly the opportunity was there. Although he knew who she was, he admitted to himself that he was beginning to like her.

Coyle was sorely tempted to let her know that he was onto her little trick just to find out what she thought she was going to accomplish. However, he realized that the medicine and fatigue prevented him from thinking clearly enough to handle a confrontation.

He reassured himself again that he had the situation well in hand. Although Lenny had insisted that he send her on her way in the morning, Coyle had about decided to let her stick around for a few days.

He knew she was lying about being a nurse, but she seemed to have enough practical knowledge to make him comfortable. All he had to do was lie in bed and take his medicine. The doctor would be checking on him daily, so she couldn't hurt anything, he reasoned.

When he got around to challenging her with the knowledge that she hadn't fooled him for a minute, Coyle knew he would need full control of his faculties. Although he wasn't about to admit that Lauren was beginning to get to him, Coyle could reluctantly acknowledge to himself that she was beginning to intrigue him.

She didn't seem the devious type, but there had to be a reason for her masquerade, and the only reason Coyle could come up with was that she'd been sent as a pretty face to woo him away from suing the pipeline.

He could concede that she was wily, but he was far from being stupid. She wasn't going to woo him away from anything, no matter how long he let her think she was pulling the wool over his eyes.

"I've lived a very ordinary life," Lauren admitted in answer to his inquiry.

"Where are you from?"

"Louisiana." Lauren saw no reason to lie about that. Louisiana was a big state.

"What brings you to Picayune?"

"A plane," she teased, hoping to divert his attention.

"Business?"

"Yes."

"Did you work at the hospital?"

"Yes." She hadn't worked at Crosby Memorial like he was probably assuming, but Lauren thought her answer wasn't actually a lie. She'd spent most of her seven years of nursing working in a hospital in Shreveport.

"And you've been in nursing a long time?"

Lauren thought the question suddenly sounded more like an accusation than a casual inquiry, but she felt he was entitled to an honest answer on that one. "Several years," she replied. "I'm an only child. My mother died a few years ago, and my father's been in ill health lately. I'm afraid most of my time is spent working or worrying about Dad," she confessed.

Coyle agreed family could be worrisome at times. He relayed a few amusing anecdotes about misadventures he'd shared with his brothers and sisters that had caused his parents to turn gray sooner than they should have.

Lauren was delighted to find that Coyle had a deep love for his family and a marvelous sense of humor.

Then, because he seemed genuinely interested in her family, Lauren told him stories about her dad and herself. As the hour grew late, she talked about her father's qualities—goodness, compassion, and kindheartedness. She told him how Cooper went out of his way to make things right when he felt he had wronged another.

In a voice that pulled on Coyle's heartstrings, Lauren confessed that she was scared that because her father had failed to take proper care of himself, he might die soon, leaving her all alone.

She talked for a long time, and Coyle was mesmerized by the silky cadence of her voice. His pain eased, and somewhere in the back of his mind, Coyle began to form an indelible bond with her, a bond that frightened him. But by the time Lauren stopped talking, the storm outside, like the one inside Coyle, had passed.

They could hear the rain trickling through the gutters into the downspouts. The air had cooled pleasantly, and the hands on the clock indicated that it was nearing 3:00 A.M.

Lauren felt emotionally drained, and she realized she no longer had the heart to carry on her deception. She cared for him too much to suggest to him that he might be at fault. She had no idea what would happen now; she just knew she couldn't go on deceiving him.

For the first time in her life, Lauren felt something remarkably close to love for a man. And, sadly, the man she chose to love would feel nothing but revulsion for her when he learned the truth. Lauren decided her only choice was to leave as quickly, and as mysteriously, as she had come. She prayed that through some miraculous act of mercy, Coyle would never find out that Cooper Vandis had a daughter.

Coyle lay silent and confused. Lauren's recitation was bothering him. Was she as vulnerable as she sounded, or was this just part of her plan to trick him? In his drug-induced state, Coyle couldn't be sure.

Lauren stood and whispered his name. Because Coyle didn't know what to say to her, he pretended to be asleep. Her hands reached out to tenderly smooth the sheet over his battered body.

Lauren struggled for a moment with an overpowering urge to place one small kiss on the angry bruise coloring his cheekbone. She knew it would be a foolish thing to do, but she knew she'd been nothing but foolish since the moment she met him.

Coyle tensed when her mouth touched his cheek as gently as a June breeze. He heard her whisper good night, flick off the light, and walk away. Then the room grew silent except for the sound of raindrops falling noisily from the eaves.

Lauren's scent, a hint of gardenias, remained in the alcove, along with one injured man wrestling with his growing confusion.

• • •

Lauren walked through the kitchen and entered her room. She picked up her overnight bag, which she hadn't unpacked, and softly tiptoed toward the doorway.

Realizing she couldn't leave Coyle without providing him with proper care, Lauren closed her bedroom door and walked across the room to search for a telephone book inside the nightstand.

It took only a moment to find the number she was seeking.

Madelyn Garrett's recorded message came through the line—there wouldn't be anyone in the office until seven o'clock the following morning, but the caller could leave a message at the sound of the beep.

"My name is Lauren, and I'm calling on behalf of Coyle Dancy." Lauren closed her eyes. "Mr. Dancy wants me to inform you that the nurse he hired yesterday hasn't worked out. Please send a new applicant to his home immediately."

Lauren replaced the receiver and took a deep, cleansing breath before slipping quietly out the back door.

Chapter Six

"YOU WHAT?"

Burke Hunter sat behind his walnut desk later that morning, dumbfounded by what Lauren had just told him.

"I know it was foolish, but I was desperate, Burke." Lauren tried to ignore the handsome lawyer's look of shocked disbelief as she continued, "I'm sure Mr. Dancy didn't suspect who I was, and, with a little luck, maybe he'll never know."

Although she'd dreaded this, Lauren knew that their company lawyer had to be informed about what she'd done. Exhausted by her sleepless night, her hasty flight to Shreveport, and the accumulated events of her past forty-eight hours, Lauren had paused just long enough to phone the hospital to check on Cooper before meeting with Burke. Because Cooper had been resting comfortably, Lauren had taken a cab directly to Burke's office before going to the hospital.

Burke picked up a pencil and studied it for a moment. "Let me be sure I understand. You flew to Picayune, went to Coyle Dancy's farm, and told him you were Lauren Vanderpool, R.N."

"That isn't a total lie," Lauren interrupted quietly. "I am a nurse."

"But you're not Lauren Vanderpool," Burke continued, ignoring for the moment her feeble attempt to rationalize her actions. "And you're telling me that Coyle Dancy hired you, never once suspecting that you were actually Lauren Vandis of Vandis Pipelines—a company Mr. Dancy, no doubt, has less than amicable feelings toward at the moment. Then you say you decided, after staying up all night with him, chatting and trying to ease his discomfort, that *you* felt that perhaps *he* had been unjustifiably wronged and that Vandis Pipelines might have been at fault in his accident. That's when you belatedly understood that you couldn't deceive Mr. Dancy any longer, so, because you realized your error in judgment, and because you were beginning to like the guy—"

"I said I sympathized with him," Lauren corrected.

She would "like the guy" if the circumstances were somehow different, but they weren't, and she'd decided not to aggravate the problem any more than necessary.

"Whatever. At any rate, come the crack of dawn, your conscience gets the best of you, and you suddenly decide you can't carry on the deception any longer, at which point you do the only noble thing you can think of—you sneak out without a word, leaving Coyle Dancy bedridden with a broken leg, two busted ribs, alone, and still under the mistaken assumption that a nursing agency had sent you to him. Do I have the facts straight?"

It sounded worse when Burke said it, but Lauren nodded. "I called the nursing service and left a message before I left. I'm sure they sent someone out first thing this morning."

Incredulous, Burke drew his dark brows together. "Why? Tell me why you would do something that . . . that . . ." Burke searched for a tactful word to describe her complete lack of responsibility.

"That stupid?" Lauren supplied lamely.

Burke's features took on a solemn expression. "That word fits."

"I'll tell you what's worse," Lauren admitted.

"There's more?" Burke gripped his pen tightly.

"I forgot to make the insurance payment."

The words hung in the air like heavy smoke on a still day.

Burke's eyes narrowed. "You what?"

"Don't you see, Burke? I did what I did to protect Cooper from losing everything he has." Lauren edged forward in her chair, hoping to make Burke understand the impossible dilemma she'd found herself in. "I know what I did was crazy, but I thought if I could have a day or two with Coyle Dancy before he found out that Vandis Pipelines didn't have a penny's worth of insurance, I could persuade him to show, if not compassion, at least a reasonable attitude toward a settlement. Instead, I discovered I couldn't carry through with the deception. Coyle Dancy has lost everything . . . and I can't help but feel we're partly responsible for it."

Burke looked as though he had no idea what Lauren was babbling about. "What makes you so sure there will be a settlement? To my knowledge, it hasn't been proved that the pipeline was at fault."

"Burke, you're not listening. I *forgot* to pay the insurance policy! Do you know what that means? It means *if* it turns out that we are at fault, Dad will lose everything he owns!"

"Wait a minute." Burke reached for a folder and flipped it open impatiently. "At approximately nine-oh-seven this morning, I personally spoke with a representative of Prattner Mutual Insurance Company concerning a possible claim. The adjuster at Prattner Mutual assured me that in the event that the pipeline was held responsible—which, may I remind you again, has not happened—that the claim would be handled promptly." Burke closed the folder and looked at her. "Don't you suppose that if the policy were still unpaid, Prattner Mutual would have brought that to my attention first thing?"

Lauren shook her head thoughtfully. "I don't understand . . . maybe there's been a mix-up and the computer hasn't caught it yet."

"I suppose it's possible, but I think it would be highly unlikely."

"Burke, I don't know why the insurance company thinks the policy is still in effect, but I'm sure it isn't. I'm positive that I didn't pay that policy. It lapsed over a month ago."

Burke placed the tips of his fingers on the bridge of his nose and studied the matter for a moment. "Any particular reason why you didn't pay it?"

"I forgot."

His left brow lifted incredulously. "You 'forgot' something that important?"

"Look, Burke—" Lauren stood up and walked toward the window "—I know it sounds unbelievably stupid on my part, but I've had my hands full the past few months trying to take care of a million things at once. If you remember, I didn't want to work at the pipeline in the first place, and you know yourself how scatterbrained I can be! Now, stop reminding me of what an idiot I am and help me! What am I going to do?"

"If what you're saying is true and the policy hasn't been paid, I'd leave town on the next banana boat if I were you."

Lauren turned and looked at him sourly. She'd known Burke Hunter since he was an intolerable eight-year-old in grammar school. Over the years they'd formed a solid, unshakable friendship built on mutual respect, but his attempts at humor sometimes fell flat. This was one of those times. "Very funny. Now tell me—what am I going to do?"

Burke sighed. "Does Cooper know the policy hasn't been paid?"

"I'm sure he thinks it has." At least Lauren hoped that that wasn't the cause of Cooper's recent heart attack. She couldn't bear to have that on her conscience, too.

"I can't believe Cooper panicked and sent you down there!" Burke exclaimed. "He should have waited and talked to me first."

"*You* were off cruising with Mary Beth Whitley," Lauren reminded.

"Mary Beth Hoskins," Burke corrected absently. "She took her maiden name back after the divorce."

"Wise choice. Mary Beth Hoskins Mitchell Anderson Whitley is a bit of a mouthful."

A slow grin spread across Burke's face. "You're just jealous of Mary Beth's adventurism."

"Please. Three divorces in eight years is not my idea of an enviable record."

"You know what you should do?"

"This better not be insulting, Burke. Remember, I help pay your retainer."

"You need to find a man and give me a break," Burke baited. "Then *he* can get you out of hot water all the time instead of me. You're too old to be running around loose."

"Look who's talking. I don't see you rushing to any altar," she returned, unaffected by his testy observations.

"Only because I don't get myself in the messes you do, *and* because I'm a compassionate person. Think of the hearts I'd be responsible for breaking if I did anything as rash as get married." He flashed her a humble smile, but Lauren ignored it.

"Well, unlike some women, when I marry, I plan to be Lauren Vandis Whatever until death do us part, so stop pushing me."

"Well," Burke conceded, turning his attention back to the weighty matter that had been thrust upon him. "You'd better give me a fast rundown on what took place in Picayune. I don't know if I can get you out of this one or not."

It took Lauren a few minutes to comply. When she was through, Burke looked pale. "Good grief!"

"I know . . . I can't believe I did it, either. Are we in big trouble?"

"I have no idea, but I'd say there's a darn good chance."

"What are you going to do?"

"I suppose I'd better start with the insurance company and see if the policy is in effect." He glanced at his watch and frowned. "It'll have to wait until I get back from Picayune."

Lauren turned from the window and approached Burke's desk cautiously while he stuffed papers into his briefcase. "Are you going to Picayune now?" she asked.

He nodded. "I have a two o'clock commercial flight. My appointment with Dancy and his lawyer is at four thirty, but I plan to return on the red-eye tonight."

"What will you tell Coyle?"

Burke glanced up. "Oh, is it Coyle now?"

"All right, what will you tell Mr. Dancy?" she said indulgently.

"As little as possible." Burke snapped the case shut. "And I'd advise you to lay low until I can get this mess under control."

"Don't worry. I'm going to the hospital to see Dad, then straight home to hibernate until this thing is settled." Lauren helped Burke slip into his suit coat.

"You'd better hope Coyle Dancy wasn't onto your little masquerade," Burke warned as he adjusted his tie. "Or the lack of insurance, no matter who's at fault, is going to be the least of our problems." Burke eyed her sternly. "I have a feeling Coyle Dancy is not going to be amused by your little deception."

"I'm sure he doesn't suspect a thing . . . but Burke, take it easy on him." Lauren's eyes softened. "He has been hurt badly."

Burke lifted his brows in surprise. "I thought his injuries weren't that serious?"

"They're not life-threatening," Lauren conceded, "but he's in considerable pain."

"Let me take care of things. Just go home and don't talk to anyone until I get back to you," Burke warned.

"Okay . . . call me the moment you get back?"

"I'll think about it."

"And Burke, be sure that the nursing agency has sent out a reliable nurse. I want Coyle to have the best of care."

Burke looked at her oddly. "What is it with you and Coyle Dancy?"

Lauren met his gaze directly. "Nothing. I just want to be sure he's being taken care of."

"That isn't your responsibility."

"Just be sure he has someone with him and that his air conditioner has been fixed."

"His air conditioner!"

"You're going to miss your plane. Just do as I ask." Lauren nudged Burke out the doorway before he could protest further. She watched as he grumbled his way through the outer office.

She had a light feeling in the pit of her stomach. It was envy. In a few hours Burke would be with Coyle . . . and she wouldn't.

In fact, it was likely that she'd never see Coyle Dancy again. The thought did nothing for Lauren's already sagging morale.

Cooper was sitting up in bed when Lauren stepped into his cubicle later that morning. Lauren was familiar with the rules of visitation for intensive care patients. Five minutes on the hour was all she would be allowed.

Cooper wasn't letting the myriad of wires and sensors attached to his chest interfere with his lunch. He was systematically spooning strawberry Jell-O into his mouth while he concentrated on the baseball game on television.

"Hi, Dad."

Cooper looked up and smiled. "Hi, Tooters."

Lauren was always moved to tears when she saw her big, robust father lying in a hospital bed, but she stifled the display of emotion and walked over to place an affectionate kiss on his cheek. "What are you eating?"

"Slop."

She grinned. "Ummm. Sounds tempting."

"Did you talk to Dancy?"

"Yes." On her way to the hospital, Lauren had mentally rehearsed what she would say when Cooper asked about her meeting with Coyle. Because of her father's condition, she obviously couldn't tell him the truth, so she'd decided to be evasive.

"And?"

Lauren smiled. "And . . . Burke's on his way right now to meet with Mr. Dancy and his lawyer this afternoon."

"Good." Cooper brought the spoon to his mouth, then swore as the left-fielder fumbled a fly ball. "Idiot!"

"Has the doctor been in today?"

"Yeah, he's in and out," Cooper said.

"Are you feeling okay?"

"Fine and dandy."

Lauren wished Cooper was half as concerned about his health as he was the game on TV.

"Have mercy! I've seen morons play better ball than this!"

"Dad, it's only a game." Lauren reached for the napkin lying on the tray and tucked it snugly around his neck.

"I don't need that thing," Cooper complained.

Ignoring his protest, Lauren opened his carton of skim milk and poured it into a glass. "I'm sorry I wasn't here when you had your attack."

Cooper eyed the milk warily. "Don't worry about it, baby. The old ticker just likes to play tricks on me every once in a while. I'm gonna be fine."

"I'm thankful we have Gloria around to take care of you."

"She's a good old broad."

"Dad." Lauren knew Cooper had the utmost respect for Gloria, but sometimes he could be rough around the edges when he referred to women.

Cooper's old grin surfaced, and Lauren was relieved to see that his color was returning. "I'm sorry. I have to admit, I don't know what I'd do without Gloria."

Lauren reached over and plumped his pillows. "You should marry her, you know."

"I know."

Lauren glanced at her watch and noted that her five-minute visit was up. "Do you need anything?"

"I'm out of cigarettes. Gloria won't bring me any."

"Good for Gloria. Lauren won't either."

"You're both killjoys."

"I'll bring you some fruit."

"Bring me a banana. At least I could hold it in my mouth and pretend it's a cigarette."

Lauren shook her head tolerantly. "Take care of yourself, Dad," she cautioned softly.

"Don't worry about me, Tooters. I'm tough as shoe leather."

Lauren shook her head and leaned to kiss his forehead.

"Oh, by the way, the insurance company called yesterday."

Lauren froze. Oh, dear. Her worst fear was about to be realized. He knew about the lapsed policy.

"Oh . . . what did they want?" She tried to keep her tone casual. If he knew about the lapsed policy, she must remain calm and do nothing to upset him further.

"You didn't return some sort of forms they sent you."

"I didn't?"

"I suppose I could have filled them out when I renewed the policy, but the agent didn't say anything about it at the time."

Her pulse jumped erratically. "You . . . renewed the policy?"

"Didn't I mention it? I saw the notice on your desk, and since the policy was about to lapse, I took a check by the office on my way to the bank that day." Cooper frowned when he saw how pale Lauren had become. "Don't you feel good, Tooters?"

"Oh, Dad . . ." Lauren sank weakly down in the chair beside his bed. The policy had been paid. She felt limp with relief.

"What's wrong?"

"Nothing. I mean I don't have the time to go into it right now. . . ."

The nurse stuck her head around the doorway. "I'm sorry. It's time for you to leave now."

Lauren nodded and stood up, her legs still threatening to buckle. "I'll be back later today."

"All right." Cooper immediately turned his attention back to the ball game. "Bring me some cigarettes if you think about it."

As she burst from the intensive care unit, Lauren clamped her hand over her mouth, forcing down her urge to giggle hysterically. The policy had been paid! The agony she'd endured for the past twenty-four hours had been for nothing.

Gloria glanced up from her vigil beside the doorway, and her face drained of color. "Oh, dear . . . has something happened?"

Lauren smiled and hugged her. "No, nothing happened. Dad's doing fine."

Gloria sagged with visible relief.

"Gloria." Lauren took her by the arm and started nudging her toward the elevators. "I'll bet you haven't eaten a bite since Dad was brought in, have you?"

"I haven't been hungry," Gloria admitted.

Punching the button for the elevator, Lauren smiled. "I'm going to buy you a sandwich and a hot cup of coffee."

Lauren's spirits were soaring. Cooper seemed to be progressing well, and now that she knew Vandis Pipelines was properly insured, the cloud of doom she'd lived under since the accident was beginning to lift.

"But what about Cooper?" Gloria's gaze went back to the doors to the intensive care unit.

"Don't worry. I'll leave word where we'll be in case there's any change in Dad's condition," Lauren promised.

"I'm surprised to see you," Gloria confessed. "Did you finish your business earlier than you expected?"

"Yes . . . much earlier."

"Then you won't be needing a suitcase sent to you," Gloria concluded.

"No." Lauren knew Gloria was curious about her sudden appearance, but she avoided meeting her puzzled gaze.

A bell sounded, and the elevator doors slid open as Lauren felt a rush of elation again. To Gloria's bewilderment, Lauren reached over and gave her another ecstatic hug. "Isn't it wonderful, Gloria?" Lauren proclaimed as the two women stepped into the crowded elevator. "Vandis Pipelines has insurance!"

After lunch Lauren went by the office to see how things were going. She was relieved to find Vandis Pipelines running smoothly under Sam's capable leadership.

Sam assured Lauren he could handle any crisis that might arise and promptly sent her home to bed.

Lauren was so exhausted by then that she didn't argue. She made a quick stop by the market to buy Cooper a large fruit basket, then went home and tumbled into bed without undressing.

The phone awakened her a little past eight the next morning. She rolled over and groped for the receiver, stunned when she saw what time it was.

"Yes," she murmured in a voice barely above a whisper.

"Lauren?"

Recognizing the voice, Lauren forced her eyes open. "Burke?"

"Did I wake you?"

"Yes . . . but I never dreamed I'd sleep through the night." Lauren sat up and pushed her hair out of her face. "What happened? Did you see Coyle?"

"Coyle is mad enough to spit nails."

"About the accident?"

"That, too. But he's mad because you walked out on him."

Lauren sat up straighter, and her mind became more alert. "Did he say that?"

"Of course he said that. Believe me, he's not a man to mince words, either."

"But he doesn't know who I am, so he's upset because the nurse walked out on him, right?"

"He's furious because Lauren Vandis walked out on him. I hate to disappoint you, dear, but Coyle Dancy knew who you were almost from the start."

"He didn't," Lauren whispered lamely, fully awake now.

"He did. Just after you left to get your suitcase, the nursing service called. When Coyle found out you were an impostor, he called his lawyer, who in turn made a few inquiries. Bingo. Guess what they came up with?"

"They couldn't have!" Lauren was astounded. Coyle Dancy couldn't have known who she was, and if he had known, why had he let her stay and make a complete fool of herself? "How could

Coyle possibly have guessed I was connected to the pipeline?"

"Lucky. And smart—Dancy's smart, Lauren, not to mention he's more bent than ever on making Vandis Pipelines pay through the nose for what he claims they've done to him."

"Oh, dear . . . if he knew who I was . . . then he must've thought Cooper sent me to con him out of suing the pipeline."

"That's about the size of it."

"But that's not so!"

"Lauren, look at the facts. The daughter of the man who owns Vandis Pipelines, a company Coyle Dancy holds responsible for ruining his life, posed as an employee of Petersen's Medical Services and *accepted* the job under false pretenses. What would you think?"

"I guess I'd think the worst, but when you explain why I did what I did, surely he'll understand."

"Which is?"

"I thought the insurance policy hadn't been renewed."

"You thought? Does that mean that now you think it has?"

Lauren felt foolish admitting it, but Burke would have to be told sooner or later. "Cooper paid it and forgot to tell me."

"Son of a—"

"Burke," Lauren warned. "I need your help. What happens now? If I can, I'd like to keep Dad from knowing about this fiasco . . . at least until he's out of the hospital and on the road to full recovery."

Burke sighed. "I don't know what to tell you, Lauren. I guess we can cover for you as long as Cooper remains in the hospital, but we've got a mess on our hands. Dancy is slapping a million-dollar lawsuit on the pipeline."

"How can he do that?"

"Easy."

"But it might not have been the pipeline's fault," Lauren argued.

"That remains to be seen. Meanwhile, thanks to you, Ms. Vandis, I've got my work cut out for me."

Lauren was confident about Burke's abilities. He had a reputation for being the finest up-and-coming lawyer around, but still . . . a million dollars. The figure was staggering.

"Won't the insurance cover the judgment if Dancy gets the amount he's asking?"

"Depends."

Lauren hated it when Burke was noncommittal. It usually meant that he was worried.

"I'll give you a ring late tomorrow afternoon," Burke said. "Maybe I'll know where we stand by then."

"All right." Lauren hung up in a daze. How dare Coyle Dancy let her make a fool of herself that way. The least he could have done was to let her know that he was onto her masquerade. At least then she would've had a chance to explain the reasons for her deception.

Instead he'd let her sit up with him all night, giving him baths and massages and pouring her heart out to him. Then the very next day he'd had the audacity to slap a million-dollar lawsuit on her! Lying back on the pillow, Lauren stared at the ceiling for a moment.

It didn't seem fair to let him get away with his arrogance, but Lauren wondered what she could do to prevent it. Coyle knew who she was. If she went back to Picayune and tried to talk to him, he probably wouldn't let her in.

But his nurse might.

Lauren sat up. Don't be foolish, she warned herself, but, even as she put on her shoes, she knew she couldn't sit still for this injustice.

Lauren had had no intentions of cheating Coyle Dancy, and he was going to hear it straight from her mouth. She would explain to him her mistake in thinking the insurance had lapsed.

She conceded that he probably wouldn't drop his lawsuit, but at least he'd have heard her side of the story.

Burke was going to murder her in cold blood when he found out that she went back to Coyle Dancy's house, she told herself sternly, but Lauren still continued to pitch her clothes into a suitcase.

She was willing to take the chance.

Chapter Seven

❖ ❖ ❖

LAUREN DECIDED to dispense with politeness this time. She rapped on Coyle Dancy's front door once and walked inside his house.

Coyle glanced up from his bed. When he recognized the intruder, his eyes narrowed with contempt. "Well, well. Look who's back."

During her return flight to New Orleans, Lauren had worked herself into a foul mood. Unfortunately Coyle Dancy was the source of her wrath.

Though Lauren could admit she'd been wrong to lie to him, she thought Coyle had been just as cold and calculating by letting her think he'd fallen for her deception.

Striding briskly to his bedside, Lauren came straight to the point of her visit. "I want to know why you let me make a fool of myself."

"Hey"—Coyle lifted one brow defensively— "don't give me the credit. You made a fool of yourself all on your own, Ms. Vandis." His tone was arrogant and unmistakably annoyed.

Lauren realized they were not alone when Elaine entered the room carrying a lunch tray.

Elaine frowned as she glanced first at Lauren and then to Coyle. "Hello . . . I certainly didn't expect to see you again."

Lauren acknowledged Elaine's greeting with a polite nod. "Elaine, I'd like to speak to Mr. Dancy alone for a moment."

Elaine glanced expectantly at Coyle, and he shrugged. "I'm not interested in anything she has to say, but since she insists on talking anyway, now might be a good time for you to pick up the new prescription the doctor ordered."

"Coyle . . . are you sure?" Elaine asked, clearly skeptical about leaving the two alone.

"It's okay, Elaine. Would you mind picking up a half gallon of butter brickle ice cream on your way back?"

"Will do," Elaine agreed, placing the tray on Coyle's bedside table and surveying Lauren warily. "You know, Lauren, Coyle's soup will get cold if you detain him for long."

Lauren stiffened her resolve. "What I have to say to Mr. Dancy will take only a minute." She was going to do what she'd come to do, regardless of Elaine's warning.

The moment Elaine left the house, Lauren descended angrily to Coyle's bedside. He flinched as she moved to plump his pillows. She appeared to grow angrier with each smack of her fist against the defenseless feathers. "I *have* never been so furious with anyone in my entire life! I told Cooper he shouldn't have sent me down here—that I would only make matters worse—but did he listen? *No,* he certainly did not!"

Coyle's eyes widened as Lauren diverted her vengeance from plumping the pillows to jerking the wrinkles out of the bottom sheet.

"Hey! Will you watch it!" He sucked in his breath as Lauren came dangerously close to jarring his injured leg. Coyle didn't have any idea what this woman thought she was doing, but he seriously suspected that she'd gone off the deep end.

"You!" She pointed her finger at him ominously. "Just be quiet."

"I will *not*." He was clearly affronted by her audacity, but Lauren didn't care. She'd flown here to tell him what she thought of him, and she wasn't going to stop until she was through.

"Why didn't you tell me you knew who I was all along?" Lauren challenged.

"Why should I?" Sensing that her fit of temper was slowly beginning to subside, Coyle settled warily against his pillows, still cautious toward her hostility. She'd better think twice if she thought she could charge in like a bull in a china shop and order him around, Coyle decided. If he were up to it, he'd throw her out on her pretty little fanny.

"I know what you think," Lauren accused, forcing herself to calm down and adding in a more reasonable tone, "you think my father sent me down here to sweet-talk you out of a lawsuit."

"It crossed my mind," Coyle agreed.

"Well, you're dead wrong."

"Dead? No, you didn't quite get the job done, lady—but you came close."

She eyed him sourly. "That isn't funny, and it isn't what I meant."

"Oh? Then I suppose you seriously think you can make me believe you weren't sent down here to talk me out of a lawsuit."

"I wasn't."

"Then why did you waltz in here and convince me you were a nurse?"

"If you'll recall, it took very little convincing. You asked me if I was a nurse, and I didn't lie. I am a nurse."

"Sure you are. And I perform brain transplants."

"I am a nurse," she insisted. "I worked in a large intensive care unit for over seven years. Is that qualification enough for you, Mr. Dancy?"

"Come off it, Ms. Vandis. You work for Vandis Pipelines!"

"I do now," she admitted. "But I haven't always."

"Personally, I don't care if you tag sheep in the Andes Mountains," Coyle said disinterestedly. "Just state your business and be on your devious way, Ms. Vandis. I'm a sick man."

Lauren eyed him harshly. "I couldn't agree more."

Coldly Coyle returned her stare. "I wouldn't

revert to name-calling if I were you. I could think of a few choice adjectives to describe what you tried to do to me, and I don't think you'd be flattered by any of them."

It was clear to Lauren that he wasn't interested in her side of the story, but she was determined that he would hear it anyway.

It was too bad the man had to be so devastatingly male, she thought. It made it doubly hard for her to concentrate on her purpose here, when her gaze kept wandering instead to his bare chest.

"Mr. Dancy . . ." Lauren perched uneasily upon the arm of the chair next to his bed. "I'm not proud of deceiving you." She deliberately avoided his indignant scrutiny. "I know you've suffered a tremendous loss, not to mention having to endure your current state of health, but my purpose for coming here was an honest and forthright one. My father's only concern was that you were comfortable. He'd wanted me to assure you that Vandis Pipelines was aware of your losses and that we were doing everything possible to return your land to its former state as quickly as we could."

"Does that mean your father can raise three bird dogs from the grave, breathe life into four thousand dead catfish, and prevent his oil from destroying my grove of one-hundred-year-old walnut trees?" Coyle countered.

"Of course not. But he can—and will—have the spill cleaned up quickly. Although we can't undo what's happened, I can assure you that you will be properly compensated for your inconvenience if it turns out that the pipeline was at fault."

"*If?* There is *no* question—your pipeline *was* at fault. And you mentioned something about inconvenience? You consider a broken leg, two broken ribs, thirty-six stitches, and losing my whole farm an inconvenience?"

This woman was the eighth wonder of the world.

"Maybe inconvenience isn't the proper word," Lauren conceded as she watched a look of sheer disbelief cross his battered features. "But it's important for you to understand that I was *not* sent down here to bamboozle you, because I wasn't."

"Then tell me, Ms. Vandis, exactly what were you trying to do?"

Lauren dropped her gaze guiltily. "Well, you see, I forgot to pay our insurance premium, and I thought that if I could win your respect and confidence before you found out that Vandis Pipelines wasn't insured, Burke, our company lawyer, and I might be able to work out some sort of reasonable settlement with you before my father discovered that I hadn't paid the premium."

It pained Lauren to admit her incompetence to Coyle Dancy, of all people, but it was a relief to be completely honest for a change.

The blood rapidly drained from Coyle's face as his head slowly lifted from the pillow. "You . . . Vandis Pipelines doesn't have insurance?"

"Oh, I was mistaken about the premium." Lauren had to quell his obvious alarm. She didn't want to upset the man any more than she already had. "I hadn't made the payment, but fortunately for everyone, Dad had paid it. He'd just forgotten to tell me about it."

Coyle's head wilted sickly back onto the pillow. He'd thought he had troubles, but he was about to decide Cooper Vandis had more of them.

"That's interesting . . . incredibly stupid on your part, but interesting," Coyle conceded. "However, it doesn't change a thing—I'm still suing you, Ms. Vandis."

I'm still suing you, Ms. Vandis! Lauren thought hatefully. Coyle's lack of sensitivity provoked her. She stood up, suddenly resigned to the fact that no matter what she said, Coyle Dancy had made up his mind to be impossible. "Sue if you must," she said, "but you're the one who'll have to live with your conscience, not me."

"I don't think I'll lose any sleep over it." Coyle wasn't taken in by her story. She hadn't paid the insurance premium, he scoffed mentally. That was just another blatant lie she'd fabricated to cover her failed mission. Well, she was wasting her breath.

"Is that all, Ms. Vandis?"

"That's all, Mr. Dancy." Lauren started toward the doorway. "But if I were you, I'd reconsider that exorbitant lawsuit. My father is not a wealthy man, nor is his health the best at the moment."

"So where is this kindly old gent who's so concerned about my welfare?" Coyle was tired of hearing about the benevolent Cooper Vandis who supposedly cared so much about another man's losses. So far, Vandis hadn't even shown the decency to contact him personally regarding the accident, and Coyle didn't have much respect for a man who would send a woman to do his dirty work.

"He's in the hospital," Lauren said softly. "Cooper had another heart attack yesterday."

Coyle's eyes narrowed. What was she trying to pull now? he wondered. Her lies hadn't worked, so did she intend to play on his sympathy? Well, that wouldn't work, either. "And I suppose you're going to tell me that his heart attack was a result of the accident?" he asked, his tone unmistakably contemptuous.

Just let him lie there, Lauren decided, and wonder if *he* was the one responsible for putting Cooper in intensive care. She wasn't about to let Coyle Dancy think otherwise.

She smiled coolly and changed the subject. "I assume the nursing service sent out my replacement?"

This time Coyle wouldn't meet her gaze. "No. Thanks to you I'm up the proverbial creek without a paddle."

"And what is that supposed to mean?"

"You lied to Madelyn Garrett for starters." He glared at her this time.

"I made it clear to Madelyn Garrett that if our agreement didn't work out, you would contact her for a replacement."

"Which, no doubt, you knew would not work out."

"I knew it would only be a matter of time until you found out who I really was." Lauren hadn't expected him to find out as quickly as he had, but unfortunately the man had the instincts of a bloodhound. Lauren reached for the doorknob, than paused. "The nursing service *did* send you a replacement early yesterday morning, didn't they?" She wasn't sure if he was deliberately trying to mislead her or not. And she wasn't sure why his care or lack of it should concern her, but for some reason it did.

"They did not. They didn't have anyone to send," Coyle snapped.

Lauren turned. "What?"

"They don't have anyone available."

"What about Mavis McCord?"

Coyle shrugged. "She's already accepted another position."

"Don't they have anyone else they can send? It doesn't seem fair they'd make you wait."

"Look, Picayune isn't Los Angeles. They'll find someone, but it may take a few days. Meanwhile, thanks to you, I'm up a creek."

Their gazes met stubbornly and held for a moment. The air grew tense as Coyle studied Lauren. "You know, if we're going to consider fairness, you're the one who put me into this position, so you should be the one who takes care of me."

Lauren lifted one brow. "I don't know how you figure that." Coyle was deliberately baiting her, and they both knew it.

Lauren wondered if Coyle knew that she had been the one monitoring the pressure on the line when it had erupted? No, she assured herself, there was no way he could know that. His remark was just an attempt to goad her into another sparring match.

"You're the one who told Madelyn Garrett the position had been filled," Coyle reminded her. "If you hadn't lied to me and to her, I'd have Mavis McCord taking care of me right now."

Lauren had to admit she felt bad about leaving Coyle without anyone to help him, but she still didn't consider it her responsibility. "Elaine appears to have your situation under control," she said. "Maybe she can stay with you until they can find someone."

Coyle shrugged again. "I appreciate Elaine's help, but she can't be with me day and night. She has her own job to manage. No, because of you, I'm virtually alone without anyone to take care of me."

"Really, Mr. Dancy." Lauren wasn't buying his phony theatrics. "Don't you have any family who can help you out?"

"No, all my relatives live in California."

"Well"—Lauren turned away—"I'm sorry, but I'm sure you'll work something out."

Coyle's somber voice stopped her dead in her tracks. "No, I won't. Why should I? I think if you honestly want to make amends for coming down here and lying to me, you'd better stick around a few days and help out . . . at least until the nursing service can come up with a replacement."

Coyle had no idea what would make him suggest such an arrangement. His attorney was right—the sooner Lauren went back to Shreveport, the better. And yet, Coyle thought it might be interesting to follow through with his original plan to heckle her a bit before he sent her on her way.

Lauren turned to face him with pained tolerance. "Surely, you're not serious."

"Of course, I'm serious. I need a nurse, and

you said that your father sent you here to make certain that I'm comfortable. Obviously, since I can't find a nurse, I'm going to be uncomfortable. If you actually have seven years of experience in an intensive care unit, you should be more than qualified to see to my needs." His gaze pinned hers imperiously. "Don't you agree?"

"My father didn't mean that I had to take care of you personally," she said curtly.

"But the point is you said you would."

Coyle began to enjoy what he was doing. If he could persuade her to stay a few days, he would show her that he wasn't one to be taken in by a pretty face and then brushed off like a pesky fly after her underhanded tactics failed. He planned to make the next few days so miserable for her that by the time she went back to her father, the Vandis family would be thrilled to pay any amount to get rid of Coyle Dancy's lawsuit.

Besides, Coyle figured, why shouldn't Lauren help him out? Wasn't she the logical one to suffer along with him since Vandis's pipelines had put him in this blasted bed in the first place?

Quietly Lauren was mulling over the situation. She knew what he was trying to do. He wanted her to wait on him hand and foot. Then, when he found someone else to do the dirty work, he'd send her on her way and smugly sit back to collect a large settlement.

On the other hand, if she did stay until the nursing service could find a replacement, she had a second chance to make him change his mind.

There was no reason why she couldn't take the job. The pipeline didn't need her. It would run fine without her—probably better under Sam Moyers's capable direction.

Cooper would be confined to the hospital for a while, and though neither Cooper nor Burke would condone what Lauren was doing, there would be little they could do to stop it.

After a few days of Lauren's personalized nursing care, Coyle Dancy would be forced to admit he'd been wrong to arrogantly assume that Lauren was an unethical schemer out to get him. Once she accomplished that, Cooper might be spared the agony of an additional lawsuit.

Lauren began to warm to the tempting thought. Though she was about to make another rash decision, this time she was certain she could make it work. She'd make the next few days so pleasant for Coyle that he'd have no choice but to get down on his hands and knees to apologize to her for his misguided assumptions.

Once he acknowledged her honesty, she could fly back to Shreveport with a clearer conscience. If Coyle still wanted to sue her father's company, at least Lauren would know she'd done everything within her power to prevent it.

"I did say I would stay, didn't I?" Lauren forced her tone to be pleasant.

"You did."

"Then I suppose it's only right that I help out until someone else can replace me."

It was all Coyle could do to keep his shock from registering on his face. He hadn't actually expected her to consent to the arrangement. Only a fool would nurse a man who was intending to bankrupt her. Coyle found it impossible to believe. "You're not serious . . . you'd actually stay here and play private nurse to me when you know what I'm going to do to you and your father the minute I get back on my feet?"

"Yes."

Coyle's eyes narrowed suspiciously. "Why?"

"Because"—she drew a deep breath—"I want a chance to prove that you're wrong about me. Once I've done that, I plan to tell you exactly what I think of you. Then I can go home with a clear conscience," Lauren revealed candidly. "And never darken your doorstep again."

"In other words, you plan to tell me to get lost once I'm able to take care of myself?"

She smiled. "I believe you've got it."

"Not a chance, Ms. Vandis." Coyle reached for the remote control to his television. "Save both of us a lot of trouble and go home right now."

"You offered me a job," she reminded him.

"Are you retracting your offer?" She could be as stubborn as he.

"I'm not retracting my offer. I'm just telling you that you're wasting your time if you think you can change my opinion of you."

"I'll take that chance. Do I have the job or not?"

Coyle grunted disgustedly and turned on the set. "Suit yourself. But you have to keep house, too."

"I thought you said you have a housekeeper," she said tightly.

"There's no sense in my having both of you here. I'll give Nellie a few weeks off."

The man was downright insufferable.

"All right," Lauren conceded, determined to remain calm in the face of adversity. "I'll have to fly back to Shreveport and make a few arrangements." She practically had to shout to be heard over the blare of the television. "Can you get by until tomorrow afternoon?"

Coyle cast her a dubious look. She wasn't serious about staying. . . . She couldn't be. "I'll try."

"Good." Lauren smiled. "I'll be back tomorrow."

I can hardly wait, Coyle thought dryly as she let herself out the door. He settled back against his pillow and began flipping idly through the channels. So, Lauren Vandis was intent on playing nurse again. He was ready to bet his last dollar that he'd just seen the last of her. She wouldn't dare come back now.

The image of Lauren in her snug-fitting jeans suddenly popped into his mind, and Coyle felt himself growing uncomfortable. He had to admit that the game they were playing was dangerous. Lauren was a good-looking woman. Too good-looking, actually, but Coyle was confident that he could keep the situation under control.

In the shape her father's company had put him, Coyle didn't figure he could make a pass at a woman if he wanted to, which he didn't, at least not with Lauren Vandis. All he wanted was to prove to Lauren that you didn't mess around with Coyle Dancy. There wasn't a remote chance that he would become personally attracted to Cooper Vandis's daughter, he assured himself. The mere thought made Coyle laugh out loud.

Coyle adjusted the volume on the television, then shifted his injured leg into a more comfortable position.

Not a chance.

Chapter Eight

❖ ❖ ❖

THE TRYING DAYS of Coyle's convalescence began, and the Dancy household fell into an organized routine under Lauren's management. Toward the end of the first week Coyle's injuries were showing considerable improvement.

Lauren glanced up from the magazine she was reading as Coyle hobbled into the kitchen on one leg. The doctor had given him crutches the day before, and Coyle was bent on becoming mobile again.

"What are you doing out of bed?" Coyle had been up twice this morning, and Lauren thought he was overdoing it.

He clumsily maneuvered his crutches across the floor and sagged limply into the nearest chair. "My sheet has a big wrinkle in it."

"Your head's going to have one in it, too, if you don't stop your whining." Lauren's tone was calm, but there was an edge to it.

She'd been here for over a week and she had to admit Coyle was the worst patient she'd ever had the misfortune to tend. At times she was certain he was doing everything within his power to make her job more difficult.

A day hadn't gone by that she hadn't threatened to leave if he didn't stop his habitual complaining. Consequently more than one heated disagreement had flared between them, but for some reason Lauren hadn't followed through on her threats.

She told herself it was because she wasn't going to appease him by leaving, and she was way too stubborn to give in to his obvious attempts to intimidate her. In spite of his foul moods, Lauren knew she was developing a fondness for him. She shivered at the thought.

Coyle frowned as he massaged his aching armpits. "These crutches are killing me."

"You've been up too often," Lauren repeated for what seemed like the hundredth time. "Naturally you'll be sore under your arms for a while."

Ignoring another one of her practical sermons, Coyle glanced around the kitchen. "When's lunch?"

"It's only ten forty-five."

"I don't care; I'm hungry."

Lauren knew the man was bored, but she'd tried everything she knew to keep him occupied. So far nothing had worked. "You're always hungry. Here." Lauren absently shoved a bowl of fruit toward him. "Eat an apple to tide you over."

"I hate apples."

"Then have a banana."

His responding sigh signaled a petulant mood coming on. "You know I don't like bananas, either."

Realizing Coyle was in another state of ennui, she closed her magazine and stood. "Okay. What would you like to eat?"

"I don't know. What are my choices?"

"Soup."

"You never get it hot enough."

"A sandwich."

"The bread's probably stale."

She looked at him crossly. "Haven't I warned you about complaining?"

"If you'd do things right, I wouldn't have to complain." When Lauren's eyes snapped him a warning, Coyle quickly decided a bacon and tomato sandwich might pacify him.

Ten minutes later the stove was splattered with grease, but the sandwich was just sitting in front of him.

"Tea?"

"No, coffee."

Of course, Lauren thought crossly, he wouldn't dare drink anything that was already prepared.

"Doesn't it seem too bright in here?" Coyle squinted as he reached for the salt and pepper shakers.

Quietly Lauren walked to the windows. As she systematically jerked the strings on the blinds, they clattered and bumped noisily against the window frames. "Is that better?"

"It's a little too dark now," he admitted as he thoughtfully studied the ingredients in his sandwich. "Where did you get this ugly tomato?"

Lauren returned to the sink. "Let me guess— it's too mushy."

"Well, if you knew that, why'd you serve it to me?" he asked impatiently. "I'm sure you could find a decent tomato if you'd looked hard enough."

"That's probably the trouble. I am not, nor do I care to be, a tomato connoisseur," Lauren stated flatly.

As Coyle glanced up, a roguish grin spread across his features. The only fun he'd had at all lately was tormenting her. "No kidding? You sure look like one."

That was precisely the problem, Lauren seethed as she began cleaning the stove. Coyle Dancy had a way of smiling at her that made her ignore the way he took such devilish delight in annoying her. His eyes were so blue that she was reminded of morning glories after a summer shower. At those moments Lauren was powerless to deal with him effectively. And she was on the verge of realizing that Coyle knew it and capitalized on it.

Coyle heaved a sigh of disgust. "I just don't think I can eat this sandwich with this tomato on it."

"Fine." Lauren walked over to the table and swiped the plate away from him, then she marched to the sink and dumped the contents in the disposal. "Heaven forbid you should have to eat an ugly tomato."

Coyle watched meekly as she took two eggs and a carton of milk from the refrigerator and slammed the door shut.

She banged a skillet down on the front burner, added a dollop of butter, and cracked the eggs open into the pan. To this, she added a few drops of milk.

Ignoring the loud racket, Coyle leafed idly through the magazine that Lauren had discarded earlier.

As she vigorously scrambled the eggs, Lauren spotted the bottle of Red Devil hot sauce sitting on the counter nearby. Casting a furtive glance toward the table, she picked up the bottle and gave the fiery seasoning several hard shakes into the egg mixture.

She switched off the burner, dumped the eggs onto a plate, and set it down before him. "See if you like this any better."

Just let him utter *one* word of complaint, and she'd walk out this time, Lauren vowed silently.

Coyle studied the eggs disinterestedly, then picked up his fork. The first bite brought a rush of blinding tears to his eyes.

Lauren crossed her arms and confronted him ominously. "Something wrong with the eggs?"

Coyle realized he'd pushed his luck too far this time. He smiled lamely. Shaking his head vigorously, he replied hoarsely, "No." His face had taken on a red glow as he meekly requested, "But I'll take that glass of tea now. . . ."

Satisfied she'd called his bluff, Lauren fixed the glass of tea and handed it to him.

A few minutes later she announced, "If you don't need anything else, I'm going to run the vacuum."

Coyle snatched up his glass. "I'll holler if I think of anything," he acknowledged between long gulps.

Lauren knew she could count on that.

Fifteen minutes later Coyle lumbered his way back into the living room. He slumped against the sofa and began rifling through the newspaper.

Sourly Lauren eyed Coyle's mountain of discarded sports sections and farm news journals as she dragged the sweeper along behind her. Ignoring his presence, she proceeded to vacuum under the sofa and around his cast.

"Am I bothering you?"

Lauren could tell by his indifferent tone that Coyle wasn't concerned in the least if he was. "Am I bothering you?" she needled back.

Coyle lowered the page of comic strips and lazily studied her outline through his half-closed lids. "Can't say that you are."

Lauren deliberately rammed his good foot out of her way and went on with the vacuuming.

"Now, now, Ms. Vandis," Coyle reprimanded in a condescending tone as he returned his attention to the paper, "are we about to pitch another one of our little fits?"

Lauren wasn't in the mood to spar with him. It must have been nice for him to have nothing to do but sit around and torment the help for the past week, she thought resentfully. She reached down and switched off the motor. As the whine died away, they both pretended to ignore the other as she picked up a dust cloth and began polishing the tables.

"Where's your hotshot lawyer today? I haven't seen him around," Coyle remarked absently as he thumbed through the classified section.

Burke Hunter had been a regular visitor at the Dancy farm since Lauren's return. Lauren didn't like to remember how furious Burke and Cooper had been when they'd found out she'd returned to Picayune and accepted a nursing position with Coyle Dancy. However, once she'd made it clear that she was staying—at least until Coyle could find a suitable replacement—they had both realized there was little they could do to stop her.

Still, Burke flew to Picayune often to make sure Lauren wasn't overstepping her bounds and jeopardizing their chances to present a proper defense for Vandis Pipelines.

He needn't have worried. Since her return, both Lauren and Coyle had artfully avoided mentioning the lawsuit.

Out of the corner of his eye, Coyle was

watching Lauren's reaction to his mention of Burke Hunter. While Coyle had to admit he'd developed a certain grudging admiration for the Vandis lawyer, he also had to confess he was beginning to feel a certain amount of resentment toward the man.

Burke had taken Lauren to dinner twice during the past week, and both times Coyle had found himself anxiously awaiting the sound of their return.

It seemed to Coyle that if Lauren was supposed to be nursing him back to health, then that's what she should be doing, not flitting around town with Burke Hunter.

Coyle was about to give up on trying to convince himself that he wasn't attracted to Lauren; he knew that he was.

But he was determined to control that attraction. Coyle was still assuring himself that it was nothing to be overly concerned about. The growing fascination would pass just as soon as Coyle was able to find a suitable replacement for her.

Lauren had come into his life at a vulnerable time. She had been by his side almost constantly since his accident, and Coyle knew it wasn't unusual for a patient to fall in love with his nurse. On many occasions Lauren had spent the long hours between sunset and dawn at his bedside, massaging his back, encouraging him in low, soothing tones when Coyle found it impossible to sleep because of his pain. It was only natural for a man in his condition to be drawn to her empathy and compassion.

Falling in love with Lauren Vandis would be as catastrophic as the accident itself, and Coyle knew he couldn't permit it to happen. But there had been times in the past few days when it had taken all the self-control Coyle could muster to keep from taking her in his arms and . . .

Lauren's voice interrupted his alarming thoughts. "I wonder where Elaine is this morning?"

Lauren wasn't overly concerned about the lack of Elaine's presence. It seemed to Lauren that Elaine had been constantly underfoot during the past week. Lauren knew the woman only meant to help, but she became piqued when Elaine insisted on taking over Coyle's afternoon back massages.

Lauren considered massages to be in her domain, and she didn't relish the idea of Elaine butting in. Lauren enjoyed caring for Coyle, and she was becoming almost possessive about her responsibility.

Coyle lowered the paper to peer at Lauren. "I hate to upset you, but have you seen the way those two have been looking at each other lately?"

Lauren shrugged. She'd noticed that Burke and

Elaine had stood on the porch and talked for an uncommonly long time the evening before. It seemed that the couple had formed an instant attraction to each other. "Why should it upset me?"

"No reason. I just thought it might."

"Well, it doesn't." Lauren was silent for a moment before she asked, "Does it bother you?"

"Does what bother me?"

Lauren turned to face Coyle. "That Burke and Elaine might be attracted to each other."

"Why should it?"

"No reason. I just thought it might," she returned.

"Well, it doesn't. I just assumed since you and Perry Mason had spent so much time together this week, you might be a little jealous of Elaine moving in on your territory."

Lauren sat down next to Coyle and began arranging a bouquet of fresh flowers she'd purchased at the market that morning. She pointedly ignored his clear-cut innuendo. "Burke and I are just friends."

"Really." Coyle looked back at the paper. "Funny, it doesn't appear that way."

Lauren snipped an inch off one stem. "What's that supposed to mean?"

"Nothing."

"Does my relationship with Burke bother you?" Lauren would have given anything if it did, but she refused to kid herself. Coyle didn't care for her; she was sure about that.

"Are you serious? Of course it doesn't."

"But it does bother you that Elaine finds Burke Hunter attractive."

"I don't care who Elaine finds attractive."

"I suppose you're just friends, too?"

Coyle lowered the edge of his paper, and their eyes met. Lauren quietly gazed into the electrifying blue depths. "Would it ruin your day if I said otherwise?"

"Not really."

"That's what I thought." He lifted the paper again. "By the way, Madelyn Garrett called while you were at the market."

Lauren felt herself tense as she always did at the mention of his finding a replacement for her. "Oh?"

"She's sending another applicant out this afternoon for an interview."

Lauren slowly rose and walked over to set the flowers on the table across the room, hating herself for feeling such a rush of disappointment. She knew it would be only a matter of time until Coyle replaced her. Wasn't that what they'd both been living for? "Maybe this one will be better qualified," she ventured bravely.

"Maybe." Coyle had interviewed four other applicants that week, but none had suited him. He slowly lowered the paper again, and their gazes met. "Listen . . ." He hesitated. Why did he feel an overwhelming urge to ask her to stay? It was almost an urge to beg her to stay, he thought miserably.

"Yes?"

As Lauren stared back at him with those wide, innocent gray eyes, Coyle's stomach wrapped into knots. He would love to kiss her, he thought, just once—just for one fleeting moment, he'd like to give in, take her into his arms, and see if she felt as warm and delectable as he'd imagined she would. His eyes unwillingly moved to the opening of her blouse. Coyle admitted how much he wanted to part the sheer fabric to taste the hollow of her neck. He imagined himself nuzzling lower to sample soft, fragrant shadows.

Coyle dragged his eyes away. "I . . . suppose I should thank you for all you've done." His voice became gruff and defensive. "I realize I haven't been the model patient."

He was cleverly adept at bringing out her tender side when he reverted to being human. "You haven't been all that bad," she said quietly. The lie was only a small one this time.

Coyle reached under one of the sofa pillows and extracted a tiny package wrapped in pink foil paper. He extended it to her timorously. "I had Elaine pick this up for me. . . . I hope it suits your taste."

Lauren accepted the package curiously. "You bought something for me?"

Coyle's eyes carefully avoided hers. "Don't look so shocked. It isn't much."

But Lauren considered the tiny gold locket to be exquisite . . . and much too generous. "Coyle, it's beautiful," she murmured, touched by his thoughtfulness. The locket was fashioned in the shape of a horseshoe and lay on a bed of luxurious blue velvet.

She could swear she saw a faint blush surface on his face, but he quickly recovered. "I thought it was nice."

She finally managed to capture his eyes. "Thank you . . . I . . . I don't know what to say."

"You don't have to say anything," he offered. "I wanted you to have the locket. You've been good to me, Lauren. . . . I know at times you haven't thought so, but I do appreciate the hours you've helped me get through. I don't know if I could have made it without you."

Lauren smiled and brought the necklace up to fasten it around her neck. "Am I about to be dismissed?"

Coyle grinned, a warm, captivating smile that made all the unpleasantness of the past week seem worthwhile. "No, in fact I've been thinking about offering you the job permanently. Would you take it?"

Her growing warmth for him shone in her smile. "Not on your life."

Coyle winked, and there was no longer the slightest trace of doubt in Lauren's heart—she was falling in love.

Burke showed up late that afternoon. Coyle watched with a jaundiced eye as Lauren took the handsome lawyer into the study and closed the door.

Trying to keep his mind off the couple, Coyle leafed through a few back issues of farm journals. He kept reminding himself that Lauren and Burke were talking business, but it didn't help his restless feeling.

Half an hour later he tossed the magazines aside and switched on the television set to watch the evening news.

The doorbell rang, and Coyle glanced up to see Elaine letting herself in.

"Hi, there!"

"Hi." Coyle turned his attention back to the news commentator.

Elaine peered around the room expectantly. "Is Burke here by any chance?"

Coyle nodded toward the study.

"Oh . . ." She eyed the closed doors enviously. "Is Lauren in there with him?"

Coyle nodded.

Elaine wandered to the sofa and sat next to

Coyle. "What do you think they're talking about?"

"I wouldn't know."

Elaine listened as the news commentator elaborated on a train derailment in the East. "Burke says he and Lauren are just friends. Do you believe it?"

Coyle didn't want to speculate. "I don't consider it any of my business."

The sound of Lauren's laughter floated from behind closed doors. As a renewed surge of jealousy enveloped Coyle, he turned up the sound on the television.

"I don't think they're just friends," Elaine confided. "I think Lauren's in love with Burke."

Coyle shot Elaine a desperate look. "So they're in love. Can we change the subject?"

"Okay." Elaine glanced wistfully toward the study again. "How are you feeling today?" she asked.

"About the same."

"Do you suppose he'll take her out to dinner tonight?"

"Who?"

"Burke take Lauren."

"How should I know? I'm not their keeper; I haven't even given it a thought." Coyle knew it was a brazen lie. He'd thought of nothing else since the moment Burke had arrived.

Elaine's gaze lingered on the closed doors as

she attempted to keep the conversation on a more pleasant note. "Did you hire the woman the nursing agency sent out today?"

"No."

"Why not?"

"She isn't what I'm looking for."

"Gee, Coyle. I've never known you to be so picky," Elaine accused. "Can't you find somebody so Lauren can go home?"

"I'm not picky—I just don't want someone around that I'm not going to be comfortable with." Coyle glanced at Elaine sharply. "Besides, if Lauren goes home, so will Perry Mason."

"Oh . . . yes, I guess he would." Elaine's gaze moved back to the closed study doors.

"Has Lauren said anything to you about wanting to leave?" Coyle asked in a tone he hoped sounded casual.

"No, but you were supposed to find someone as soon as possible," Elaine reminded him.

Coyle shrugged. "What can I tell you? I'm looking, Elaine. That's all I can do."

Elaine lay her head back on the sofa wearily. "I get the distinct impression you aren't in any hurry to replace her."

Coyle was uncharacteristically silent as he stared fixedly at the set.

"Are you falling in love with her?"

"I get the distinct impression you're the one in a hurry for me to replace her," Coyle accused, ignoring Elaine's question. "This wouldn't have anything to do with you and the lawyer, would it?"

Sitting up straighter, Elaine sighed. "It might. Why don't you like Burke?"

"I didn't say I didn't like him."

"If you ask me, he's being extremely nice about the lawsuit, Coyle."

"I didn't ask you."

Elaine sat up as an infectious grin spread across her face. "Coyle Dancy, you're jealous."

"I am not."

"You are! For the first time in your life, you're actually jealous. *You're* falling in love with Lauren Vandis, aren't you?"

"Get off it, Elaine. I'm not jealous, and I'm not falling in love with Lauren." Coyle snapped off the television and reached for his crutches. "Haven't you got anything better to do than let your imagination run wild? I'm going to the kitchen."

Elaine was still laughing as Coyle hobbled irritably into the next room.

In love with Lauren Vandis, Coyle thought disgustedly. Elaine had lost her marbles.

Burke and Lauren were cloistered for over an hour. When they emerged from the study, Lauren was laughing. Her smile faded when she saw Elaine waiting on the sofa.

"Elaine, how nice to see you." Burke enthusiastically crossed the room to greet the attractive brunette.

"Hello, Burke." Elaine's smile was warm as she clasped his hands eagerly.

Lauren glanced around the room. "Where's Coyle?"

"In the kitchen."

"I'll check on him." Lauren sensed that Burke would appreciate a moment of privacy with Elaine.

Lauren found Coyle standing at the window, staring out at the approaching storm. Low rumbles of thunder sounded ominously from the west. The sight of his tall frame silhouetted against the window caused a familiar tingling.

Straightening her shoulders and her resolve, Lauren moved to the opposite side of the kitchen. "Sounds like it's going to rain again," she said as she opened the refrigerator. "Want something to drink?"

"No."

Lauren filled a glass with ice. The crystal cubes popped and cracked as she poured tea over them.

"I don't think the air conditioner is working right," she remarked. "We may have to call the repairman again."

"Do whatever you think."

"How did the new applicant work out?"

"I didn't hire her."

"Oh?" Lauren took a sip and closed the refrigerator door with her hip. "Why not?"

"I didn't want her, okay?"

Lauren was beginning to suspect that Coyle was deliberately stalling about hiring another nurse. The applicants the nursing service had sent out had all been qualified to take her place. But it didn't matter; she wasn't anxious to leave.

Still, she could tell something had put Coyle in another foul mood. Shrugging, she decided to ignore it. "Okay. Maybe the next one will work out."

Lauren started to leave the room when the sound of Coyle's voice stopped her. "Lauren, come over here."

Another rumble of thunder rolled through the kitchen as Lauren paused in the doorway. "Do you need something?"

For a moment she thought he hadn't heard her. Coyle stood gazing out the window as the first drops of rain began to fall.

He had his back turned to her as she approached him. "Did you need something?" she asked again.

Slowly Coyle turned to face her, and Lauren was surprised to see a look of inflexible determination on his face.

"Come closer," he prompted softly. "You may have to help me out."

"Closer?" Her mouth curved into an unconscious

smile as she stepped forward. Lightning flashed at the window, illuminating the darkened room. "All right, I'm closer."

He was acting strange. Lauren's pulse fluttered irregularly as Coyle reached out and gently touched her face. The unexpected, tender gesture made the blood run warm through her veins.

His eyes caressed her face with unabashed longing. "I'm about to do a very foolish thing," he confessed in a quiet voice. "And I sincerely hope you won't be inclined to retaliate by breaking my other leg."

"I seriously doubt you're in any immediate danger," she said indulgently. "What is this terrible curse you're about to put on me?"

"I'm going to kiss you," he announced with a remarkably staid calmness.

"And you think I might object?"

"I don't know. It's crazy. It'll solve nothing, and it'll only complicate matters more, but since I can't get it out of my mind, I guess I'm going to have to do it."

Lauren wasn't sure if she had just been insulted or complimented.

"I have to agree—it won't make things any easier." Lauren tried keep her tone noncommittal, though her insides were quivering with anticipation. Coyle was right. It would be crazy if they became involved romantically, but it was a madness she'd felt was inevitable from the very beginning.

Coyle's earlier decisiveness suddenly seemed to waver. "I . . . we could really turn this thing into a mess, couldn't we?" His troubled eyes sought hers imploringly, sending a silent plea for her to stop him.

But Lauren wasn't going to. She nodded. "It could get real sticky." She felt like such a traitor to Cooper. Falling in love with a man bent on destroying her father was not the smartest thing she'd ever done, but she'd done it.

He swore irritably. "Well, what do you think we should do? I can't keep ignoring the fact that you're a desirable woman, Lauren. Either I have to do something about it, or you're going to have to walk out on me."

Lauren lowered her eyes. "I could never do that."

Coyle ached to take her in his arms and protect her. She could look so vulnerable at times. "Then how are we going to handle it?" Coyle edged closer. He was only inches away from her now. "I'm getting sort of used to you . . . you know . . . in the night." His eyes ran over the outline of her lips. "I admit I like having you here, Lauren."

"Well," Lauren took one step, and her arms came up to encircle his neck. She gazed into his eyes as the pleasant scent of soap and aftershave filled her senses. "Then maybe you'd better keep me happy."

The resulting look he gave her was so galvanizing, it sent a tremor racing through her like a brushfire. "I was sort of thinking the same thing." He winked. "Do I have any limitations?"

She shook her head.

His eyebrows lifted with surprise. "You're kidding? I'm the heel who's suing you—remember?"

"Listen, cowboy . . ." Lauren pressed closer against him, and both their bodies tingled with the contact. "Are you going to just talk about it, or are you going to kiss me?"

Two adorable dimples appeared on his cheeks that she'd never noticed before. "Eager, huh?"

"Just curious," she defended.

Chuckling, Coyle took her chin in his fingers, then slowly brought his mouth down to taste hers.

The contact was a delicious, heady sensation.

Closing her eyes, Lauren parted her lips and let the intoxicating domination of his mouth capture hers.

"Not bad, Ms. Vandis." Coyle's breath was warm as his mouth moved up to explore the outline of her ear.

"Not bad at all, Mr. Dancy," Lauren admitted, as her arms crept around his neck and their mouths came together hungrily.

With a soft moan, Coyle brought her to his chest as the kiss deepened in intensity.

A brisk rap sounded at the doorway, and Coyle and Lauren jumped apart guiltily as the kitchen door suddenly swung open and Burke poked his head around the corner.

"Hey. We're going after a bucket of chicken . . . oops!" Burke quickly assessed what was happening, then murmured apologetically, "Sorry, I didn't mean to interrupt anything."

Nervously Lauren brushed a stray lock of hair out of her face. "Don't be silly, Burke." Her flushed features betrayed her obvious attempt to cover up the incriminating scene. "We were just about to have a glass of tea. Will you join us?"

Burke shot Coyle a sharply appraising glance, and the two men exchanged a brief, but unmistakable message.

Burke warned Coyle to leave her alone.

Coyle urged the Vandis attorney to mind his own business.

Burke asked again, "Do you two want to share a bucket of chicken with Elaine and me?"

Lauren glanced expectantly at Coyle.

Coyle shrugged. A bucket of chicken was not exactly what he had in mind. "Sounds okay to me."

Lauren smiled at Burke appeasingly. "Chicken sounds good, Burke. I'll fix a salad to go with it."

Burke disappeared behind the door as Coyle and Lauren finally looked at each other.

Their faces suddenly broke into grins.

Coyle lifted his brows and mouthed incredulously, "Chicken?"

Chapter Nine

❖ ❖ ❖

"IF IT WERE I, I'd build bigger ponds this time."

Slowly Lauren ran her fingers down the set of figures Coyle had used when he'd constructed his ponds the first time. Her head drew closer to his as she continued, "If you use larger drainpipes, remove all the stumps and obstructions, and smooth the bottom this time, you might be able to improve your chances of having a more profitable harvest."

It was shortly after seven on a Saturday evening. Lauren and Coyle were sitting on the front porch, relaxing and enjoying the magnificent sunset about to take place.

The round orange ball of fire lay low on the western horizon, and the air quickly cooled from a stifling one hundred and two to a more tolerable ninety-six degrees.

It was hard for Lauren to believe that she'd been in Picayune for nearly a month now. Coyle's house was beginning to feel more like home to her than the three rooms and a bath she sublet in Shreveport.

The weeks with Coyle had flown by, weeks when it had become easier for their hands to touch, their lips to steal kisses, and their eyes to meet and linger longer than was necessary—or wise.

At times like this, Lauren realized that her resolution to remain immune to Coyle's magnetism was melting away like snow on an April morning. Whenever her hand accidentally brushed his, or whenever they verbally sparred with each other—as they too often did—Coyle could suddenly put a stop to their arguing by pulling Lauren into his arms and masterfully kissing her into breathless submission. Those occasions always made it extremely hard for her to remain indifferent.

Still Lauren couldn't help but sense that a deep well of suspicion still existed in Coyle. It was almost as if he were afraid to place his trust in her.

Lauren found herself torn between wanting to prove to Coyle that she had no ulterior motives for caring for him and continually reminding herself that despite what she was feeling, she couldn't allow herself to become emotionally involved with him. She was painfully aware that a binding relationship between them would be impossible because of the circumstances that fate had thrust upon them.

At least she could console herself with the knowledge that Coyle had been honest with her. His lawsuit had been filed and was scheduled to go to trial sometime in late October. Because of Cooper's health, Burke had been granted a change of venue, and the trial would be held in

Shreveport. Lauren dreaded the hour. The outcome of the lawsuit was in serious doubt. Burke planned to produce evidence in behalf of Vandis Pipelines that stated the ruptured pipeline was clearly indicated on Coyle's deed. Coyle's lawyer would produce documents showing Coyle Dancy's deed stated the pipeline was located in the exact *opposite* end of the property. Obviously an error had been made in the abstract. Both parties had a strong case.

When Coyle had announced the court date, that familiar stubborn light had entered his eyes, but now Lauren sensed that he no longer took joy in what he was doing. It seemed that Coyle simply felt that he'd been wronged and that the party responsible for his misery was going to pay—even if it meant he'd have to oppose Lauren, too.

Lauren understood Coyle's feelings; sometimes she even found herself sympathizing with him. She'd seen the agony he was going through. Still, she was torn between wanting to shield her father from financial chaos and experiencing abject frustration as she continued to fall more deeply in love with the man who could do irrefutable harm to Cooper.

Lauren continually struggled to retain an air of detachment from Coyle, but she knew she couldn't go on denying her feelings forever. The underlying, electrifying attraction she felt for him was a dangerous current that threatened to sweep her along in its wake at any time.

Lauren wasn't sure what she was going to do, but she knew time was running out. Although she hated to admit it, she knew her choices—she could either leave immediately or be prepared to stand with Coyle against her father when the case came to trial.

She knew she could do neither.

So each day Lauren delayed her inevitable decision, hoping some miracle would come along to alter the situation. So far the miracle had failed to materialize.

Coyle was sitting in a glider across from her with his injured foot propped atop an old lawn chair. A pitcher of freshly squeezed lemonade was close at hand.

He leveled blue eyes on her, clearly surprised by her knowledgeable observations on catfish farming.

"So that's what you'd do, huh?"

Lauren nodded as she reached for her glass. "Of course I know very little about raising fish."

"I'm shocked you know anything about it at all," Coyle confessed. He thought it was unlikely that anyone who'd forget to pay an important insurance premium could be familiar with the intricate details of ichthyology.

"I've read most of the material you have lying around," she confessed.

Coyle leaned back, a slow grin settling on his rugged features. He had to admit that he admired Lauren Vandis. "So, what do you think I should do about replacing the fingerlings? Should I go with the smaller ones that I can buy at a better price, or should I pay premium for the large, well-fed ones?"

"You want my honest opinion?"

Coyle nodded, a little surprised to discover that he honestly did want her views.

"I think the meager savings you'd realize from buying the smaller fish would be lost several times over if disease breaks out or if their growth is slow and inconsistent."

"Is that a fact?" His grin widened admiringly.

"It's my humble opinion." Lauren reached for his glass to refill it. "But then, who am I?"

His look grew somber. "Yeah, sometimes I wonder who you really are."

"You know who I am," she reminded him gently, aware of the underlying skepticism creeping into his voice.

His sigh sounded wistful. "I wish I could be sure." But then his tone suddenly lifted as he said, "You know, it's a shame about us. If circumstances were different, I might ask you to marry me."

His words hit Lauren like a bombshell. This was the last thing she'd ever expected him to say. Her startled eyes flew up to meet his twinkling ones, and she realized that Coyle was goading her again.

Nevertheless his flirty innuendo made Lauren's heart pump a good deal faster.

"I could use a good-looking blonde with your fish savvy around here," he admitted.

Reminding herself that she wasn't going to read anything serious into what he was saying, Lauren settled back against her chair and gazed up at the saffron-colored sky. "Yes, our situation is sad. I'd probably even be silly enough to give your proposal serious thought—if our circumstances were different."

It surprised both of them to find they could speak lightly about their situation. Lauren thought maybe they were finally making progress.

They sat for a moment, sharing a compatible silence while Lauren savored the idea of Coyle actually saying "I'd like to marry you" and meaning it someday. It was a foolish fantasy, but Lauren found she liked the warm way it made her feel. Coyle would never feel that way, she reminded herself. He was still halfway convinced that she was staying just to cajole him into dropping his lawsuit, but weeks ago she'd given up trying to persuade him otherwise.

Coyle finally broke the quiet interlude. "I suppose Burke's with Elaine again tonight?"

Lauren nodded, and her mouth curved into an unconscious smile as she thought about the romance blossoming between Burke and Elaine. Burke had flown the company plane to Picayune so many times in the past few weeks that Lauren was sure it could find its way on its own by now.

Each time after a brief, perfunctory meeting with Lauren, Burke would immediately seek companionship with Elaine Tarrasch. The lawyer and the realtor made a striking couple, one that reportedly turned a number of heads everywhere they went. "I'm beginning to suspect that for the first time in Burke Hunter's life, he's falling in love," Lauren confided.

"He couldn't find a nicer woman to fall in love with," Coyle admitted. "Maybe at least one good thing might come out of all this," he mused softly.

"I hope so."

Silence overtook them again as they lost themselves in their own convoluted meanderings. The sun dipped low and slid lazily over the horizon. The cicadas began their nightly serenade, filling the air with their loud, shrill noises.

"How's your dad feeling?" Coyle's voice brought Lauren out of her pleasant reverie.

Coyle knew that the reason Lauren flew back to Shreveport every Saturday was to visit her father. However, except for the first night after her return to the Dancy farm, Lauren had never mentioned her father to Coyle, and yet he'd sensed that the two must be very close.

Lauren was touched by his polite inquiry. She knew Coyle had swallowed some pride just to make the simple gesture. "He's doing very well, thank you," she replied in a soft voice.

"Is he out of the hospital yet?"

"Yes, Dr. Franks even says Dad can go back to work next week."

Coyle mumbled something under his breath that sounded unfairly disparaging to Lauren.

"Coyle, I'd like to pinch your head off sometimes," she chided. "Dad is a wonderful man. You'll see for yourself, once you meet him."

"Meet him?" Coyle cocked one brow at her wryly. "You must be kidding. I'm the last person your father would want to meet."

Lauren felt strange openly discussing the one subject that they'd so meticulously avoided lately, but she knew that they couldn't go on avoiding it forever. "I'll admit Cooper isn't thrilled about the lawsuit, but he isn't a man to hold grudges either. If the court decides in your favor, then Dad will accept the decision."

"I'll bet he will."

She glanced at him expectantly. "What will you do if you lose?"

"I'm not going to lose."

Lauren sighed. Coyle Dancy could be as stubborn as a ten-alarm fire at times. "Let's suppose that on the wildest, most improbable chance the court fails to rule in your favor," Lauren reasoned, meeting Coyle's gaze straightforwardly as she asked, "will you hold a grudge?"

"I will."

At least he was honest, Lauren thought as she averted her gaze. "That's too bad. In the end bitterness will only end up hurting you."

"Lauren," Coyle said with just a touch of patience in his voice this time. "I have to win. If I don't win, I'm bankrupt. Would it make you and your father happy to see me bankrupt?"

"Of course not, but I don't know why you insist you'll be bankrupt. The insurance company will replace your actual losses," Lauren argued. "I'm sorry, but I think the additional million-dollar lawsuit against my father is unwarranted, Coyle."

"You wouldn't be just a little prejudiced, now would you?"

"Not at all. I think I'm able to see both sides quite clearly."

"Sure you do," he agreed with skepticism clearly ringing in his voice. "I'm sorry we're on opposite sides of the fence, Lauren. I need that extra money to get me on my feet again."

"I've been more than willing to try to see it your way," she offered. "But I'll admit I don't understand why anyone would sue over something that was an accident. Accidents happen, Coyle. Unfortunately, life isn't foolproof. And cases like this are exactly why insurance rates are so astronomical!"

Coyle shot Lauren an impatient glance as she unconsciously climbed atop her imaginary soapbox.

"Why, even doctors are being forced out of practice because they can no longer afford to pay liability insurance," she declared, warming to a subject she'd kept bottled up too long. "What are the poor and homeless going to do for medical care? Nowadays people grossly abuse their privileges in the name of justice, and then become outraged when they discover they, too, can no longer afford the insurance premiums. Someone has to put a stop to it." Her eyes were blazing as she came to an abrupt halt.

"Well, it's not going to be me, so forget it."

Lauren shook her head in resignation. He was impossible.

In stubborn silence, Coyle struggled to ignore her reasoning. Lauren was entitled to her pious attitude, but she wouldn't coerce him into dropping his lawsuit. *She* wasn't the one who'd lost everything she owned. *She* wasn't the one slapped flat on her back for who only knew how many weeks. Lawsuits were the American way, and until the day Lauren Vandis had come into his life, Coyle had thought they were a pretty good idea. Anyone with any sense at all would do what he was doing, Coyle thought defensively.

"I think we'd just better drop the subject," Coyle finally admitted. "We obviously don't view the situation in the same light."

"All right . . . but you're wrong."

"Let's drop it."

"All right, all right. I won't say another word on the subject . . . but you're wrong."

Lauren settled back on her chair and felt a pang of disappointment when she realized how much she was going to miss the moments she shared with Coyle, even though they couldn't agree on anything as simple as the time of day. What would she do when she could no longer talk with him, see his smile, share a part of his life?

As if he could read her thoughts, Coyle asked quietly, "And what if circumstances between you and me were different?"

At first Lauren wasn't sure how she should answer. Her fingers went absently to her throat to touch the gold locket. Should she act coy and pretend to misunderstand his question? That would be foolish, she decided. She understood perfectly well what he meant, so she chose to answer with total candor. "If circumstances were different . . . it would make me very happy."

Coyle became reticent as twilight began to lengthen the mysterious shadows. It would have been easier for him if Lauren had answered otherwise because it would have dashed all hope of their getting together someday. This way, she only made him want something he knew was out of the question. Lauren Vandis was there to fleece him. Was he going to let himself be suckered in by her pretty face and her great set of legs?

Coyle turned to Lauren with every intention of making it clear that he wasn't interested in her, when their eyes suddenly met and held. They stared at each other for a long moment, then Coyle swore softly as his head involuntarily moved toward hers.

Wordlessly their mouths met.

It was the opportunity Lauren had been waiting for. She slipped out of her chair and eased carefully onto his lap.

The kiss grew abruptly ardent, and Coyle wasn't happy with the rapid change of course. This was the last thing he'd planned to happen.

"Careful of the ribs," he complained, which made them both chuckle. Suddenly the tension between them evaporated into thin air.

"Do you think I would hurt you?" Lauren scolded tenderly.

Coyle's breathing unwillingly quickened as he caught Lauren's hands. "What are you doing?"

Gently loosening from his hold, Lauren smiled. "Just relax. I'm not going to bite you." She spoke with a quiet firmness as their mouths came back to meet each other's. "Well, maybe just a tiny bite," she corrected as she began to nip playfully at his earlobe. "Here . . . here . . . and here. . . ."

"Come on, Lauren, this is going to get us both in trouble," Coyle admonished. "Stop it."

"Make me."

"Good grief, Lauren!" Coyle rebuked gruffly as he firmly grasped her arms and tried to push her away.

She grinned repentantly.

"You have nice hair," she complimented him, devilishly teasing a springy curl around her forefinger. She grinned when she saw a disapproving scowl cross his features. "And nice eyes . . ." Her fingers traced the outline of his lips, "and an incredibly tempting mouth. . . ."

"Come on, Lauren, cut it out." Coyle shifted around in the glider uneasily. "What if someone sees us?"

Lauren tilted her head sideways to survey the vast open spaces of the Dancy farm. "Who would see us?"

"How should I know? Someone could . . ."

She laughed, ignoring his warning and pressing her nose tightly against his. "You're a hopeless grouch. Maybe another kiss will help."

"You're asking for trouble, lady," Coyle warned gruffly as she pulled his head down to steal another forceful kiss.

"Then why disappoint me?" she tempted.

Coyle's voice trailed off helplessly as his mouth claimed hers in an almost frightening act of possessiveness.

Suddenly the playfulness was gone. Their kisses took on a sense of urgency as Coyle gave in to his desire. Lauren began to tremble as she recognized his surrender.

Breaking the embrace, Coyle's eyes moved over hers with unspoken longing as his hand came up to cup her face. Whatever differences stood between them, they seemed momentarily meaningless and no longer worth the agony of depriving himself of what he could no longer deny he wanted most: Lauren.

"What are we going to do about this?" he prompted softly.

Gazing into the inner depths of his eyes, Lauren found her answer remarkably easy. "We . . . need to admit our feelings."

Passion deepened the blue in Coyle's eyes to a dark indigo as he pressed his nose against hers intimately. "I'm a man . . . you're a woman . . ."

"Oh, Coyle . . ." Lauren laid her head on the broad width of his chest and closed her eyes.

"I suppose we should go inside," Coyle observed.

"Might not be a bad idea."

"Coyle." Lauren placed her hands on his face, and her eyes shown with love. "This is right, you know . . . incredibly right."

His smile was tender as he gazed back at her. "I know . . . it just scares me."

She grinned. "It'd better."

"Lady, you are downright wicked," he accused as he bent his head to press his lips against the pounding pulse in the hollow of her throat. "Just the way I like a woman."

Lauren closed her eyes, savoring the sensations suddenly swelling inside her.

"You're beautiful," she confessed as her gaze wandered admiringly over him.

She knew she'd embarrassed him when she saw the shy grin that followed.

This was exactly how it should be, she thought.

She smiled at him. "There may be hope for us after all." She felt no shyness with him, only a need to please.

Would he think she was still trying to outmaneuver him?

Lauren prayed not. She loved this man . . . loved him with every fiber in her, and the situation was out of hand. She couldn't play this game any longer.

"Coyle?"

"Yes?"

Lauren decided what she had to do. Come morning, she would leave him and fly back to Shreveport. It would be unthinkable to try to remain detached—especially now. She loved him so much her heart felt bruised. She needed time away from his intoxicating presence, time to try to find an answer to their problem. Though he had never said so, Lauren knew Coyle loved her just as deeply as she loved him, but should he end up losing the lawsuit, Coyle Dancy's pride would be a hard thing to reckon with.

He was able to get around on his own now, and with the help of a capable housekeeper, he would do fine without Lauren.

Tonight had proved another thing to Lauren. Coyle Dancy would forever hold a place in her heart, no matter how the lawsuit was decided.

Leaning over, he pulled her to him, and their mouths met in another long, meaningful kiss. Seconds stretched into long minutes before they could bring themselves to break the embrace.

"If you'll give me a few minutes, I'll think of better things to do than talk," Coyle offered as he absently smoothed her hair with his large hand.

Lauren caught his hand and pressed it tenderly to her lips. She didn't know how she'd ever find the strength to leave him—but she would.

"Do you feel like taking a walk?" she asked.

Coyle chuckled and patted his cast. "How about a five-mile sprint instead?"

"I mean it, Coyle. I want to show you something."

Realizing she was serious, Coyle smiled. "Okay. Where are you dragging me?" Coyle complained good-naturedly as they made their way through the kitchen and out the back door. "Remember, my arms are still sore from these crutches."

"How could I *ever* forget?" she deadpanned dramatically.

It took a while to reach their destination. Coyle was complaining loudly when they finally arrived at the site where the accident had taken place.

"I thought you said it wasn't very far. . . ." His voice died away lamely as he realized where she'd brought him.

It was the first time Coyle had been to the site since his accident. Lauren watched his face grow somber as he leaned against a fence post to view the barren ground. The moonlight seemed only to magnify the complete desolation.

"Why are we here?" he asked.

Lauren winced at the agony in Coyle's voice, but he had to know before she left. She gave him a few moments to catch his breath before she stepped over to wrap her arms around his waist and squeeze him tightly. Standing on tiptoe, she kissed him.

The affectionate gesture served to temper Coyle's momentary edginess. "What's going on?"

"I think you should see something."

"What?"

Lauren walked to a large walnut tree and carefully parted the thick brush surrounding it. She leaned down and picked up the small, broken stake that had once warned of the presence of the pipeline, and extended the evidence to him dispassionately.

For a moment Coyle stood in stunned silence. He thought, *that pipe had been marked.*

Finally, after what seemed like hours to Lauren, Coyle asked in a remarkably calm voice. "How long have you known?"

"For weeks. Burke and our insurance adjuster discovered it a few days after the accident," Lauren admitted softly.

Anguish flickered briefly across Coyle's face. It tore her heart to see the way he was looking at her—as if she had personally betrayed him.

"Coyle . . ." Lauren stepped toward him, wanting to ease his distress. "It doesn't mean you've lost the lawsuit," she reminded him gently. "It only means the pipeline was marked. . . ." Her voice trailed off helplessly as she watched his eyes return to the sign.

"You've known for weeks?"

"It's possible."

He leveled his eyes on her, eyes that earlier had openly adored her. His look told her that it was all he could do to tolerate the sight of her. "So, the joke's on me, huh?" he concluded. "You've been hanging around just so you and your hotshot lawyer could see how big of a fool you could make out of me."

"That's not true. I've been 'hanging around' because I care what happens to you, Coyle."

"Right. Well, we'll see who has the last laugh." He turned, then paused. "I think it's time for you to go home, Lauren."

His words were like a lance driven straight through her heart.

He started to limp away as Lauren bolted forward. "Coyle, wait. . . ." Hot tears started down her cheeks. "You're not being fair. I only want you to consider the possibility we might have both been at fault. You were probably preoccupied that morning and failed to notice the marker. It was small. . . ."

"You should have mentioned your marker an hour ago."

"Coyle . . . please." What they had shared had been priceless. She couldn't let him think it had meant nothing to her . . . that he meant nothing to her. "Don't do this. . . ."

If he heard her, he didn't stop and he didn't wait.

At that moment, as far as Coyle was concerned, Lauren Vandis didn't exist.

Chapter Ten

❖ ❖ ❖

"IF YOU'RE SO crazy about the man, then why did you leave him?" Burke poured a cup of coffee and placed it firmly in Lauren's hands. "Drink this. You look like heck."

"Thanks. That's just what I wanted to hear."

"I didn't mean to insult you, but you're going to have to get yourself under control, Lauren. We can't go into court tomorrow looking like martyrs. We've got an uphill battle the way it is," Burke reminded her. "I promise you, the men and women of the jury are going to sympathize with Coyle. Jurors identify with a working man who sustains injuries and losses like Coyle's. They tend to favor the little guy over the large company. Besides, people figure that corporations have all the money in the world anyway."

"I know that, Burke," Lauren agreed unemotionally, "and I promise you I won't do anything to hamper our defense."

"Good. See that you don't." Somewhat satisfied with her answer, Burke lowered himself into the high-backed leather chair behind his desk. He picked up a pencil and rolled it absently between his fingers as he studied the sad expression on the pretty blonde sitting opposite him. "You take the cake—you know that?"

Lauren's shoulders lifted helplessly.

"Now you've fallen in love with Coyle Dancy. What next? You plan to marry the guy?"

"He hasn't asked."

Burke's brows lifted in mortification. "And if he does?"

Lauren calmly set the cup of coffee on the edge of the desk. "Don't worry, he won't."

"Look . . ." Burke leaned over and handed Lauren his handkerchief as tears began rolling silently from the corners of her eyes, "everyone makes mistakes. You're going to make yourself sick if you don't stop this."

Trying to force a denial around the goose egg suddenly forming in her throat, Lauren finally gave up and covered her eyes with the handkerchief. Seconds later she was weeping openly as Burke discreetly waited for the storm to pass.

When it did, he speculated gently, "Coyle hasn't called you since you got back?"

Lauren nodded mutely as she tried to stem the flow from her eyes.

"That's strange. I'd have sworn he would have."

Lauren glanced up hopefully. "Why? Have you seen him?"

"Occasionally. Elaine feels sorry for Coyle, so she's asked him to join us for dinner once or twice." Burke turned away from the love shining brightly in Lauren's eyes.

"Is he okay?" she asked.

Burke shook his head. "You've got it bad, haven't you?" he asked, looking back at her.

Ignoring his sympathy, Lauren prodded softly again, "Is Coyle all right, Burke?"

"He's doing fine. The doctors removed his cast last week and replaced it with a smaller one. Coyle went home and threw his crutches away. He's walking with a cane now."

Lauren's mouth curved with affection as she pictured Coyle pitching the despised crutches into the trash. She only wished she could have been there to help him. She buried her face in the handkerchief and burst into tears again.

"Does he have someone helping him?" she asked between muted sobs.

"Just Nellie. Lauren, you've got to get a hold on yourself." Burke stood up and poured water into a glass, then handed it to her. "He won't hire another nurse. He insists he doesn't need one."

Lauren felt a surge of elation at Burke's admission. Maybe Coyle missed her after all. "Has . . . has he mentioned me?" she prompted, hoping Burke had overlooked telling her before.

"No . . . but then he hasn't been good company lately." At the rapid resurgence of tears in Lauren's eyes, Burke added gently, "Lauren, that doesn't mean he isn't thinking about you. He's just so testy that no one wants to be around him.

Look, if you're so miserable, why don't you call him? He flew in this morning for the trial."

"Never!" Lauren banged her hand down angrily on the corner of the desk.

Burke leaned forward, disturbed by Lauren's attitude, yet powerless to change the circumstances that had brought it on. "Why not? Are you going to spend the rest of your life crying every time someone happens to mention Coyle Dancy?"

Lauren's shoulders stiffened with renewed resolve. "If I have to."

"What do you want from Coyle, Lauren? If you're looking for him to drop the lawsuit, you can forget it. He's going to see this thing through to the bitter end."

"Burke . . ." Lauren edged forward in her chair. "Exactly what are Coyle's chances of winning?"

Burke shrugged passively. "He'll get a chunk. I hope it won't be in the neighborhood of what he's asking, but due to the mix-up on the deed, I fully expect the jury to side with him."

Lauren was quiet for a moment, trying to assess the probable damages. "What will that do to Dad?"

"It won't bankrupt him. His business is healthy—it will bounce back."

"The jury will find for Coyle even though the pipeline was marked?"

"It's possible."

"Then Coyle could win."

"That's my guess, but anything can happen," Burke reminded her.

"I don't want Dad hurt, but I don't want Coyle hurt either," Lauren confessed.

Burke pitched the pencil onto the desk disgustedly. "Women! If I live to be a hundred, I'll never understand the way they think. If you're that much in love with Coyle Dancy, you'd better take the bull by the horns and phone the man."

"If Coyle Dancy had wanted to talk to me, he would've called me by now!" Lauren flared. "Apparently he isn't half as concerned about my welfare as I am his!"

"Then what's the problem? Sounds to me like you're better off without him."

"You're absolutely right." Lauren sniffed as she dabbed angrily at her eyes. She'd lived a perfectly happy life until she'd had the misfortune to meet Coyle Dancy, and if she had to, she could live without him.

"Can you accept that and finally get back to normal?" Burke inquired in an expectant tone.

Lauren's face suddenly crumpled again. "Noooo . . ." She buried her face in the damp handkerchief and began sobbing again.

Defeated, Burke reached for the thick folder marked "Vandis Pipelines." He moved down the list of witnesses he had scheduled to appear the following morning, and with an efficient stroke of his pencil, he drew a line through Lauren's name.

Observing his action out of the corner of her eye, Lauren sniffed. "What are you doing?"

"Nothing . . . just making myself a note." Burke closed the folder, and his smile was pleasantly dismissing. "In case you change your mind, Coyle's staying at the Ramada."

Lauren glanced up petulantly. "Which one?"

Burke told her and added, "Just in case you're interested."

Lauren opened her purse and drew out a small pearl compact. She opened it and dusted powder onto her red nose. "Don't be silly. I wouldn't call that wretch if I were drawing my last breath."

"I don't blame you." He scribbled a number on a notepad, then ripped off the sheet and handed it to her.

Lauren scanned the phone number, then lifted her gaze back to Burke. "What's this?"

"The number of the Ramada."

It was all Burke's fault, Lauren thought miserably. If he hadn't told her that Coyle was in town, she would have been content to wait until the next day to see him. Now she couldn't get him out of her mind.

Lauren sat in a restaurant that evening, staring at her untouched meal. She had stopped briefly to see Cooper and had decided to eat before she went home.

She wondered what Coyle was doing. Had he eaten? Was he alone in his motel room . . . and lonely? No, she decided, Coyle would probably be stretched out, eyes glued to the television set . . . or, she mused, perhaps he was wondering what she was doing? Lauren quickly dashed that hope. She told herself that Coyle was probably gloating over the fat settlement he was going to make off Cooper now that the case was coming to trial.

The injustice of it all made Lauren burn. Still, she couldn't deny that in a small corner of her heart she actually wanted the court to award Coyle a settlement. But she still harbored a tiny hope that he might, at the last minute, drop the lawsuit.

Her appetite completely gone, Lauren laid down her fork and stared out the window at the passing traffic. She wanted nothing from Coyle Dancy but his love. Hadn't every unorthodox action she'd taken since the accident proved that to him?

Although Cooper had been forgiving when she'd run off to take care of Coyle while he, too, had spent his days in a hospital bed, Lauren knew that her father had to wonder about her loyalties.

A little voice inside Lauren nagged at her—if

Coyle won his lawsuit, as Burke predicted, would she still feel the same about Coyle, knowing he didn't care enough about her to make personal sacrifices of his own?

The answer was still yes, but it didn't make Coyle's betrayal any easier for Lauren to accept.

As she walked to her car, she tried to justify Coyle's actions, but it didn't ease the hurt of knowing that he simply hadn't cared enough about her. True, he'd lost everything, she conceded, but why did he have to try to take her down with him?

Two wrongs did not make a right, Lauren reasoned, as she got into her car and inserted the key into the ignition. And she would burst if she didn't get to tell Coyle so.

She was making mistake number two thousand and four, she warned herself, as she pulled the Fiero into the line of traffic. Or was that two thousand and five?

Coyle answered his door on the second knock. For a brief instant, when Lauren first saw him— tall, dark, and incredibly handsome—standing before her, she felt an urge to throw herself into his arms and beg him to drop the suit while there was still time.

She was ripped apart by longings. She wanted to smother her loneliness inside the shelter of his arms; she wanted to be held against that broad chest; she wanted him to devour her mouth and beg her never to leave him again. She wanted to . . . but her eyes began to tear when she remembered the reason she'd come to see him.

Fool that he was, Coyle was willing to throw away all that they had shared in the past few weeks just to win his precious lawsuit. For a second Lauren was tempted to shake some sense into him.

Coyle's features softened when he saw Lauren standing in the doorway. Wordlessly, he stepped forward, his arms reaching for her.

But his eyes widened when Lauren suddenly flung her savings passbook at his chest. "Here, Mr. Dancy! You might as well take every penny I have, too!"

Dodging instinctively, Coyle groaned when he heard his neck pop. As his hand came up to grasp the spiraling pain, he glared at Lauren. "What do you think you're doing!"

"Giving you *all* of the Vandis money. Isn't that what you want?"

Glancing warily at a group of people who'd paused to listen, Coyle grasped Lauren's arm and dragged her into his room. After slamming the door shut, he turned to confront her. "Where have you been?" he demanded crossly. "I've been trying to call you."

"Really," she said dryly. "For three weeks?"

"Not for three weeks," he snapped, but his flare

of temper began to abate as he drank in her familiar sight. "I've called your apartment every fifteen minutes since I got in this morning."

"Oh?" Lauren faced him coolly. *Why* did he have to look so good? she agonized.

His face was nearly healed, with only one or two tiny red marks to attest to the accident. Barely using the cane to support his lithe frame, he stood straight and tall, towering over her.

Memories of their last night together haunted her, but she quickly summoned sarcasm to mask her pain. "It hasn't bothered you to let three weeks go by without calling me, so what's the big hurry now?"

"Lauren, I've had a lot on my mind, okay?"

"No, it's not okay. You could have at least picked up the phone to let me know you were still alive." Lauren could feel her emotions teetering, and she warned herself to leave before she made a bigger fool of herself. But Coyle was so near . . . so close . . . so male!

Coyle's voice softened. "Will you pipe down? I'm ready to talk now."

"Sorry, but I'm out of the mood now."

Coyle's sluggish shrug wasn't encouraging. "Fair enough. I guess it's up to me to get you back in the mood."

Sweeping her into his arms, his mouth came down to capture hers in a hungry, magnetizing kiss that rocked Lauren to her inner depths. She gasped softly, and the storm gathered force as she wrapped her arms possessively around his neck.

Their kisses felt like charged electrical currents. Lauren's heart literally skipped a beat as the kiss deepened.

"Coyle Dancy, this is crazy," she protested. "I came here to tell you what I think of you . . . not to . . ." Coyle's mouth stopped her confused reasoning with a dominant kiss.

"You can tell me what you think of me later," he promised. "Give me a chance to change your opinion."

She reached to stop him. "It won't have the intended effect later," she pleaded.

He grinned, a boyish, captivating gesture that sent her pulse racing feverishly. "I know." The tip of his tongue touched the palm of her hand provocatively. "That's my only hope."

How was she to think straight with this sort of sweet madness? "Coyle . . . I . . . we need to talk."

"You just said you didn't want to talk," he reminded her.

"I've changed my mind. Coyle . . ." His mouth returned to hers, nibbling first, then coaxing a response from her.

She sighed and surrendered to his embrace.

"Lauren . . . my lovely, lovely little Lauren, stop fighting me, sweetheart. I've missed you. . . ."

His husky, heartfelt whisper brought about

Lauren's complete undoing. The weeks of separation fell away as he whispered her name and gently pressed his lips to her forehead. Coyle knew he could never, in one lifetime, get enough of her.

"Oh, my darling, I've missed you. . . ."

She heard the soft intake of his breath as her mouth began to explore the sinewy ridges and warm skin around his neck, eyes.

"Lauren . . . there's so much I want to say to you. . . ."

"I know . . . shhh . . . I know. . . ."

"Coyle?" She wanted to stay in the haven of his arms and forget they hadn't solved a thing.

"Uhhh?"

She smiled as her finger lazily traced the outline of his jaw. His eyes were closed peacefully.

"I came here to tell you what a rotten, no-good, despicable louse you are."

"Uh-huh . . . I better warn you, you won't be the first." He opened one eye cautiously. "But go ahead if you think it'll help."

"Coyle Edward Dancy . . ." She sighed. "I think you're a rotten, no-good, despicable wretch, and I hate what you're doing to us."

"What is it you think Coyle Edward Dancy's doing?" he asked. He made a mental note to ask her how she knew his middle name.

"By continuing with your lawsuit, you're ruining any chance we could ever have for a meaningful relationship."

"Well, pardon me, but I thought the last few kisses were quite meaningful," Coyle rebuked.

"That's the problem," Lauren seethed. "It seems you're perfectly content to love me, while I'm foolish enough to want more."

Coyle sighed heavily. "How much more?"

"What?"

"How much more do you want? Twenty minutes—half an hour? Exactly how much time would it take to make you completely happy?"

Lauren snorted disgustedly. "I don't know why I torture myself over you. You're not worth it."

"That depends on who you're talking to."

Lauren sat up and eyed his mischievous grin sourly.

His grin died a sudden death. "You know," he said, "you have a real irritating way of jumping to conclusions. How do you know what I think or what I want?"

"I think it's pretty obvious you don't want me. You've told me on more than one occasion what a wicked little schemer you think I am."

"Aw, forget what I said. I was just hacked off."

"And you haven't called since I left—"

"Walked out on me," he corrected.

"Walked out on you! You asked me to leave, and you sure didn't seem to mind when I did."

Coyle was silent for a moment. "I did mind. I just didn't want to admit it . . . even to myself."

"Then why didn't you call?"

"Why didn't you call me?"

"I didn't think we had anything to say to each other."

"That's why I didn't call you," he confessed. "But that doesn't mean you haven't entered my mind a time or two lately."

Lauren found small comfort in his vague admission. "Well, I suppose we're star-crossed lovers. . . . Perhaps it's time you knew that I was the dispatcher on the line when it erupted. It'll come out in court tomorrow anyway."

Coyle knew. "Sounds like something you'd do—blow up fish, kill my dogs, ruin my life."

"*It* wasn't my fault. *You* were digging the ditch."

"Hey, I thought you'd given up trying to talk me out of the lawsuit."

"I have."

Coyle chuckled with male superiority. "Then you're finally admitting that that's what you've been up to all along? I thought so."

Chapter Eleven

❖ ❖ ❖

"ALL RISE."

The occupants of the small room came to their feet as the judge entered the court from his chambers.

After seating himself behind the bench, he rapped the wooden gavel and briskly brought the session to order. "Is the plaintiff ready to state his case?"

Lenny Baxter's deep voice rang out clearly. "The plaintiff is ready, your honor."

"Is the defense prepared to do the same?"

"It is, your honor."

"You may proceed."

Lauren sat down and deliberately turned her back to the plaintiff's table. She was determined to ignore Coyle, who was sitting in his chair looking like a wounded warrior. His limp had seemed more pronounced when he'd entered the courtroom, and he'd added a neck brace since she'd seen him the night before.

"Dad, are you comfortable?"

"I'm fine, Tooters." Cooper smiled at his daughter fondly and added, "Relax, this shouldn't take long."

Lauren thought her father was remarkably calm for a man who was about to be taken to the cleaners. She patted Cooper's hand affectionately and turned her attention to the proceedings.

Burke leaned closer and whispered in a tight voice, "Why is he wearing that neck brace?"

"Who knows," Lauren returned crossly. "It's probably some sick gimmick he and his lawyer thought up to get the jury's sympathy."

Burke glanced at Lauren, then he looked away, then back at her again. "Why are *you* wearing sunglasses?"

"I . . . I have a headache," she murmured.

Lauren was afraid to remove her dark glasses because then everyone would see her red eyes. She'd spent most of the night crying over that miserable phony wearing the neck brace.

"Take off the sunglasses. The judge is going to think he's dealing with a bunch of fruitcakes," Burke grumbled impatiently.

"No, Burke, the glasses stay," Lauren snapped. She would die if Coyle saw the evidence of her misery. She'd almost convinced herself that he wasn't worth one tear, let alone a bucketful, until she'd caught a glimpse of him getting out of the taxi an hour ago. Memories rushed back to remind her that the only one she was fooling was herself. No matter how cold-hearted he was, she still was hopelessly in love with him.

"Your honor, I'd like permission to approach the bench." Everyone watched as Lenny Baxter rose to his feet.

Judge Waterman patiently motioned for him to do so.

"What's he up to now?" Lauren whispered anxiously as Coyle's lawyer began to confer with the judge in hushed tones.

"We'll see," said Burke.

The judge looked up and directed his words to Burke. "The plaintiff has requested a meeting of the attorneys in my chambers."

"The defense will be happy to comply with the plaintiff's request, your honor."

Burke laid his pencil down and stood up. "Oh, boy." He took a deep breath, then remarked to Lauren and Cooper under his breath, "I hope this means what I think it does."

Lauren eased forward. "What? . . . What do you think it means, Burke?"

"Just hold your horses." Burke tugged on the sleeves of his suit coat.

"The court stands recessed for thirty minutes." The judge banged his gavel, then rose and gathered his papers. Moments later he disappeared into his chambers with the two attorneys trailing in his wake.

"What do you think they're talking about?" Lauren asked again as she and Cooper walked toward the coffee machine in the corridor. She removed her sunglasses, but kept them close at hand.

"Oh, you know lawyers. They always have

their legal mumbo jumbo to go through." Cooper dropped a quarter into the machine and punched the button that indicated coffee with heavy cream and heavy sugar.

Lauren viewed his selection distressfully. "I thought Dr. Franks told you to avoid cream."

"He did, but I can't drink coffee without it. How do you take yours?"

"Black . . . with a little sugar."

Cradling steaming cups in their hands, Cooper and Lauren began their anxious wait as the large clock on the wall moved with agonizing slowness.

Once or twice Lauren noticed Cooper fumbling in his shirt pocket for a cigarette, only to discover his pocket was empty.

Lauren smiled encouragingly at him. "I'm proud of you, Dad. How long has it been since you had your last cigarette—two months?"

"It feels like two years," Cooper complained. Moments later he announced he was going to the newsstand to get something to chew.

Lauren did a double take when Cooper returned five minutes later with a package of chewing tobacco in his hand.

"Dad!"

Cooper looked startled. "What's the matter now? I'm not smoking."

"But you're chewing!"

"But I'm not smoking!"

Lauren could see that Cooper clearly failed to see the connection.

Ten minutes later Coyle emerged from the courtroom in conversation with two other men. He paused for an instant as Lauren's eyes met his. She quickly averted her gaze, and he limped along beside the others as they continued down the hallway in the opposite direction.

Watching Coyle move away made Lauren's heart ache. Were they doomed to always be on opposite sides?

"Lauren, are you all right?" Elaine Tarrasch stepped over and pressed a clean tissue into her hand. Lauren hadn't realized she was crying again.

"Thanks, Elaine." Lauren took the tissue and wiped guiltily at her eyes. Cooper mumbled something about talking to someone and wandered away, leaving the two women to talk in privacy.

"I hate to see you and Coyle tearing each other apart like this," Elaine confessed. "Is it really worth it?"

"I'm not the one bringing the lawsuit," Lauren reminded her.

"Lauren . . ." Elaine reached out and took her hand. "Coyle is in love with you—surely you know that."

"He doesn't act like a man in love."

"Coyle has a stubborn streak a mile wide; you

know that. He's really mixed up about you right now."

"He shouldn't be, Elaine. It's up to Coyle to decide what's more important to him—his precious lawsuit or me. I'm not sure I even want him. . . . I'm sorry, Elaine. I just can't talk about it right now."

Lauren whirled and walked away, fighting to regain her composure. She knew she was only kidding herself again. She wanted Coyle Dancy; she wanted his love and devotion; she wanted a reprieve from this madness.

It was an hour and ten minutes before the judge appeared in his courtroom again. He called the court to order, and his gaze traveled around the room before resting on the people sitting at the defense table. In a clear voice he announced, "The plaintiff has requested that the attorneys negotiate an out-of-court settlement. In compliance with the plaintiff's request, I am dismissing the case of *Dancy versus Vandis Pipelines*."

There was a shocked silence before the courtroom erupted in a round of applause. Lauren sat silently staring at her folded hands. She knew she should feel nothing short of elation. Instead she felt slightly sick to her stomach.

"Tooters?"

"I'll be with you in a minute, Dad."

Cooper squeezed her shoulder encouragingly. "I'll wait for you outside." Cooper left Lauren sitting alone as the courtroom rapidly emptied.

Drawing a deep breath, Lauren lifted her gaze to stare at the ceiling fan, which was laboring hard to move the stagnant air around the room. Where was the thrill of victory? she wondered. It was sadly missing. All she felt was an overwhelming sense of guilt that she'd just helped to cheat the person she loved most in the world.

Because Coyle loved her, he would settle for probably half of what he could have gotten in court. Worse, she realized, was that the amount would probably be half as much as he was actually entitled to.

Lauren felt ashamed, sad, and every bit as underhanded and conniving as Coyle had accused her of being. If she hadn't stormed into his life, if she hadn't wanted him to fall in love with her, if she hadn't cried, begged, pleaded, and coerced him, he wouldn't have dropped his lawsuit today.

She dropped her head. A lump the size of Iowa was crowding her throat. Lauren was reaching for a tissue when she heard a man clear his throat. Looking up through a veil of unshed tears, she saw Coyle standing near, looking down at her.

Dropping her gaze, she said softly, "Thank you."

"For what?"

"For . . . giving in to me."

"Giving in to you?"

"Stop it, Coyle. You know that's what you did . . . and you shouldn't have. You deserved to win."

"I know."

She looked up to meet his gaze.

"Just as long as *you* know that," he corrected in a stern voice.

"You shouldn't have let me browbeat you like I did."

"I wasn't aware that you were browbeating me."

"Maybe I didn't mean to, but you knew I wanted you to drop the lawsuit."

Coyle shrugged. "You're entitled to your own opinion. I shouldn't have taken my anger out on you and your dad. I should have been willing to settle for damages, and I should have tried to put my life back together instead of sitting around waiting to get rich from my misfortune."

"You know your decision means that you lose." Earlier, it had seemed so important to him to come out the winner.

"I guess it depends on how you look at it." He placed his hand gently on top of hers. "The way I have it figured, I've won—big-time."

His tenderness started tears rolling from her eyes. "How could you possibly figure you've won? The accident—"

"If there hadn't been an accident, I wouldn't have met you," he said softly. "And if I'd never met you, I would've missed the best thing in my life."

"Oh, Coyle . . ." She was practically sobbing. "You know your decision means you'll probably get only half of what you might have gotten."

Coyle sat in the chair next to her and set his cane aside. He reached up and removed the neck brace.

"Why were you wearing that thing?" Lauren asked, snapping out of her self-pity long enough to scold him. She couldn't see why he would have tried to play on the jury's sympathy if he'd planned to settle out of court anyway.

"Because an ill-tempered woman I have the misfortune of loving threw her savings book at me."

Lauren's face flushed sheepishly. She'd completely forgotten about her childish behavior the night before. "You're such a pansy."

"And you're such a pain in the neck—literally." They looked at each other and grinned.

"You hurt my feelings last night," she told him.

"I'm sorry, but it's your fault. Like I said, you've jumped to too many wrong conclusions about me, Lauren."

"I don't know *what* to think of you, Coyle. You won't let me get close to you."

Coyle lifted one brow wryly.

"You know what I mean," Lauren accused. "Why did you let me go on thinking you didn't love me?"

"Did I say I didn't love you?"

"You never said you did. The way you let me leave last night without saying a word about where we'd go from there certainly made me think you didn't."

"Well, maybe we should discuss that right now. Where do you think we should go from here?" Coyle asked.

"Well . . . I don't know. Where would you like to go from here?"

Coyle looked at Lauren and gave her an outrageously suggestive wink.

Lauren lifted one brow imperiously. "Am I to assume that you're asking me to marry you?"

"Sounds good to me."

"Maybe I won't."

"Why not? Something wrong with marriage?"

Her eyes met his lovingly. "No . . . it's wonderful." She wanted to kiss him. No, she wanted to do more than kiss him. She wanted to devour him.

Coyle's blue eyes softened with indistinguishable love. "I love you, okay? I'm crazy-head-over-heels-can't-live-without-you. All right?"

His exaggeration brought the beginnings of a smile to her face. "All right."

"So, instead of hashing this thing around, why don't you come over here and kiss me hello?" His tone was suggestively inviting, and Lauren didn't hesitate.

She moved to his chair and sank into his waiting arms. Their mouths merged as he kissed her deeply.

How long he'd loved her he wasn't sure. He just knew that now he loved her more than life itself.

"Hello," she whispered when their lips parted for a moment.

"Hello, Tooters."

Her eyes widened. "Tooters!"

"That's what your dad called you." Coyle grinned.

Lauren was horrified that Coyle had discovered Cooper's embarrassing nickname for her. "When did you hear him call me that?"

"Last night."

"Last night? You talked to my father last night?"

"For a couple of hours," Coyle confessed. "You were right—I do like him. He's a heck of a nice guy."

Lauren couldn't imagine why Cooper hadn't told her that he'd talked to Coyle. "What did you talk about?"

"You, mostly. I asked him if he'd have any objections if I asked you to marry me. . . . Of course I thought he might—in view of all that's happened—but he said if I wanted you, I should have a go at it."

"He said that? Was this before or after I saw you last night?"

This barter between the two men in her life didn't seem very flattering or glamorous to her, but, on second thought, Lauren figured, it sounded exactly like something Cooper and Coyle would say to each other.

"Hours before." Coyle pulled her mouth back to touch his as his voice dropped into a husky whisper. "I think you ought to know I offered to drop the lawsuit altogether, but Cooper wouldn't let me."

"Why?"

"He said if I had my heart set on marrying you, I was going to need all the help I could get."

Lauren pinched his cheek capriciously. "You lie."

"I do not. We sat down, and it took is over an hour to figure how much Cooper could afford to pay without hurting himself—and making me look like a fool. We finally came up with a healthy sum, which I'll quietly accept when Burke offers it to me. Then I'll put that healthy sum away in a nice little trust fund for Cooper's future grandchildren. There's only one clause in the agreement."

"And that is?"

Coyle gathered her possessively. " 'Son,' Cooper said to me, 'I want you to father those children.' "

Lauren grinned. "Don't I have any say in the matter?"

Coyle shook his head. "No, we have it all settled."

Noting her look of consternation, Coyle pointed out, "You'd only screw it up, honey. I plan to take care of you from now on."

Realizing he'd returned to his favorite pastime of goading her, Lauren playfully boxed him under his chin. "I can't think of anyone I'd rather have father my children, even if you are an old grouch."

"Good, because we're going to spend"—he kissed her again deeply—his tongue sent shivers of anticipation racing up her spine—"long nights working on that project."

"Is it close to dark, yet?" Lauren couldn't remember when she'd ever been so happy.

Then it all finally sank in—Coyle had known last night that they had every chance of making their relationship a lasting one, but he'd tried his best to make her think he was going through with the lawsuit. She was going to have to have a long talk with him later.

"I can't believe you and Cooper would actually be in cahoots with each other," Lauren chided. "Burke will have a fit!"

"Burke will never know," Coyle warned. "Coop and I made a pact. This is between him and me."

"Coop?" So it was Coop now.

Coyle winked at her again. "Believe me, honey, he's going to make a good father-in-law. You know, we're a whole lot alike."

Lauren hadn't wanted to admit it, but she'd harbored the same unnerving suspicion for weeks.

"You amaze me."

"I plan to—for at least the next sixty or seventy years." Coyle eased her from his lap and reached for his cane. "Which reminds me, we have a plane to catch."

"Where are *we* going?"

Coyle shot her a look of pained tolerance. "Didn't I mention we were getting married today?"

Stunned, Lauren shook her head.

"Oh . . . I'm sorry. We're flying to Vegas with Burke and Elaine tonight. Burke thought it might be nice to make it a double ceremony . . . but that's up to you. We'll have our own wedding if you prefer."

"Have I agreed to marry you? Or is this another little matter I have no say in? I don't have to agree, you know," Lauren said, picking up her purse and walking out of the room with him.

She wouldn't miss that plane if she had to crawl on her hands and knees to the airport, but it wouldn't hurt to let Coyle know that she still planned to keep the upper hand.

Coyle's footsteps paused, and his cocksure manner suddenly threatened to desert him. "You will marry me . . . won't you?"

"Of course, I will."

Coyle's shoulders wilted with relief. "I thought you would, but I was prepared to argue with you about it. I'm getting pretty good at winning our arguments."

Lauren supposed it wouldn't hurt to go on letting him delude himself.

He shot her the most devastating grin and looped his free arm through hers. "By the way, do you think you'll like raising catfish?"

"No."

Coyle laughed. He *loved* this woman! He pulled her ear closer to his mouth and whispered in a seductive tone, "Then how do you feel about the prospect of being my woman?"

"Now that's different," Lauren conceded as they emerged from the courtroom arm-in-arm. "Dancy's woman. I'm going to love every moment of it."

Center Point Publishing
600 Brooks Road ● PO Box 1
Thorndike ME 04986-0001 USA

(207) 568-3717

US & Canada:
1 800 929-9108
www.centerpointlargeprint.com